Model Horse

Model
Horse

JENNY HUGHES

BREAKAWAY BOOKS
HALCOTTSVILLE, NEW YORK
2013

Model Horse
Copyright © 2013 by Jenny Hughes

ISBN: 978-1-62124-002-0
Library of Congress Control Number: 2013935004

Published by Breakaway Books
P.O. Box 24
Halcottsville, NY 12438
www.breakawaybooks.com

NOTE: For this edition, we have Americanized the spellings (for instance "color" instead of "colour"), but kept the original British vocabulary and usage. So, for anyone not familiar with some of these terms, here is a brief list with their American equivalents: rosettes= ribbons; downs=open fields with rolling hills; mate=friend; copse= a small group of trees; head collar=a horse's halter; numnah=saddle pad; school=riding ring; yard=stable area.

10 9 8 7 6 5 4 3 2 1

Chapter One

I saw the muscle in Limelight's silver-gray shoulder twitch suddenly and I tensed immediately. He turned his fine head, nostrils flaring, dark eyes wide as he surveyed the quiet countryside. Perched nervously in the saddle, I tightened my grip on his reins and silently prayed for calm.

In the few weeks I'd owned him the glorious, showy pony had become increasingly hyper, shying at every unexpected sound or movement—or worse, bolting off uncontrollably. I knew I should relax, soothe him with voice and body language, but the truth is I was becoming scared—very scared. I tried to bring him back to my hands, to slow the pace to a smooth working trot instead of this maddening, highly strung jig-jogging. I think I was beginning to win but just as he dropped his nose a loud shot rang out, reverberating around us. In one movement Limelight snatched at the bit, stuck out his neck, and lurched into gallop, whipping the plaited leather through my fingers so fast I could feel friction burns.

Somehow I stayed on board, crouched in my stirrups, as I fumbled frantically with the useless reins. He was veering sharply to the left and I did my best to give-and-take with my right hand in an effort to both slow and straighten him. The only effect it seemed have was to make the whole thing more terrifying—Limelight carried on galloping flat-out, now swerving violently one way while his head faced the other! It was a bit like traveling at top speed on a runaway roller coaster—no brakes, no steering, and little chance of a soft landing. We'd left the track way behind, thundering across scrubby grass and rough undergrowth, and were now, to my horror, heading for a wood. I stopped my useless tugging on the right rein so that at least the bolting horse would look where he was going and thought briefly about jumping off. It wasn't an option: Not only would I most likely break a leg, but Limelight would be panicked even further, causing injury to himself and maybe others. Beyond the trees, the main highway was not too far away, and I knew I had to stop him before he reached it. The sky suddenly darkened as we ducked under the canopy of trees;

he was still galloping, despite having to weave in and out of the closely packed trunks. I did everything I could with seat, hands, and voice but he wasn't listening, just running. The thin, whippy ends of branches lashed my face, my legs were scraped painfully against tree after tree, and a horrible choking feeling of terror constricted my throat.

Somehow Limelight crashed and snaked his way through the small copse, and again I did my best to stop him before he could take off in the open. He fought me defiantly, sticking out his neck and leaning on the bit, using all his superior strength to keep me from regaining control. My arms and legs were exhausted, it was all I could do to stay in the saddle, and when I saw a sedate line of ponies ahead I could only groan aloud. I tried my hardest to turn him away from them, this time using right leg and left hand in an attempt to steer round the group of riders. I nearly made it, but at the last minute Limelight shied violently to the right, carting me helplessly through the middle of the group of ponies, who promptly scattered wildly in every direction. I heard an enraged shout and shrieked in reply, "I'm sorry, I'm so *sorry!*" as my horse and I bludgeoned our way through and vanished up the hill, leaving a horrible mess of frightened riders and skittering ponies behind us.

Still Limelight galloped headlong and I was very, very aware that we were heading straight toward that highway. Desperately, using both hands and every last vestige of strength, I again heaved to the left, gradually pulling him off the track toward a solid-looking bank of bushes. Still he fought me but now he was tiring, and with a crashing of twigs, small branches, and prickly leaves we met the shrubs full-on, the impact sending me over the gray horse's head where I lay, spread-eagled and winded on the broken green mass. Limelight stopped too, having absolutely no choice, half his body wedged inside the bushes with just his handsome rump and long, silky tail sticking out.

Trembling, I scrambled to my feet and grabbed his reins before he could free himself and take off again. For a while we just stood there, with me in a complete state of shock as I shakily stroked Limelight's sweat-slicked neck to try to calm him. Somehow I managed to back him up and get him out of the shrubbery, but there was just no way I could climb back into that saddle. Instead I walked beside him the entire way to the Marcus Equestrian Center, where I kept this brand-new horse of mine. It was more a hobble than a walk, in fact. My left knee was stiff and swollen from being cracked against the trees, and although I didn't remember bashing it my right ankle was throbbing in protest. As we approached the stables at the center, I could see a small figure by its gate, peering anxiously up and down the road.

"Hannah!" Even my voice sounded pathetic, and I could see the concern on my best friend's face as she rushed toward us.

"Casey, are you all right? You look terrible!"

"I feel terrible." I had to swallow hard so as not to burst into tears.

"Raine says you and Limelight just came crashing through the middle of her ride. They were all beginners—she said you caused chaos." Hannah put her arm round me. "Did he take off with you again? You're both hurt so—"

"No, Limelight's okay. It's just me," I said dully.

"Your face is all scratched up and you're limping badly so I thought your horse must be hurt, otherwise you'd be riding him."

I couldn't bring myself to admit I'd been too scared to

remount. "My knee was so sore I couldn't get back on. Is Raine really mad at me?"

Hannah gave me another kindly hug. "I said Limelight must have bolted but she seemed to think he was just playing you up—says you shouldn't be riding out if you can't control him."

Raine is the owner of the equestrian center, nice enough, but a strict disciplinarian who likes everything just so.

"She's being hard on me because she's still mad I bought Limelight without consulting her," I said sulkily. "Raine wanted me to get some quiet little thing trained to do exactly what he's told, when he's told."

"Well, you sure can't put Limelight in that category!" Hannah was trying to cheer me up. "Come on, Casey, there's no harm done—your leg will heal, your horse is fine, and none of Raine's novices actually fell off."

We'd at last reached the center gates. Stiffly, I led Limelight through to the yard and his stable, wanting nothing except to go home and soak in a hot tub for an hour. Horses' needs always come first, though, so I started untacking my wayward pony, grateful for Hannah's help as she trotted around returning the saddle to the tack room and fetching my grooming kit and the fat hay net I'd got ready. I'd scraped off all the sweat, washed Limelight's legs, and covered him with a light stable rug before I heard Raine's voice outside and knew I was in for trouble.

"They're back then?" She spoke sharply to Hannah. "I'm surprised Casey's got the cheek—I've never seen such an irresponsible display of riding in my life!"

"I'm really sorry." I limped to the door and looked her in the eyes. "I didn't mean to upset your ride. There was a bang—some hunter out shooting I guess—and it scared Limelight."

"Scared nothing!" She was really, *really* mad. "That crazy horse of yours was having a whale of a time."

"No, I swear he bolted." I felt my voice shake. "I nearly steered him round you but something else made him shy—"

"Nonsense. He bucked and swerved, playing you up and disobeying you. I told you the minute you bought him the horse is totally unsuitable, and the only thing you can do is get rid of him. He needs an experienced rider who can sort him out."

"I've been riding here since I was eleven," I said hotly.

"That's four years' experience and I'm *not* going to get rid of him as you put it. I love Limelight."

The silver-gray pony rubbed his head gently against me as if he'd understood. I slid my arm round his neck and held him tight.

"Oh, Casey." Raine's face softened a little. "I can see you love him but he's green, he's very high-spirited, and you've only ever ridden my properly schooled ponies, who are a different can of worms altogether."

Yeah, I thought defiantly. *They're well trained all right, but they're docile and—and BORING!*

Aloud I said, "I'll really work on the schooling, Raine, I promise."

"You'll have to." The tough look was back. "Because until you've got some semblance of control, I'm barring you from riding out across the common. You and Limelight are too dangerous; those young kids with me today could have been badly hurt because of you."

"What! So I can only ride in the school?" I couldn't believe she could do this, and I said as much to my parents when I finally limped home.

To my dismay they did nothing to back me up.

12

"Look at you, Casey." My mum stuffed my dirty, green-stained clothes in the washer. "Your face and hands are covered in scratches, you can barely walk, and you admit Limelight frightened the life out of you. I spoke to Raine the other day and I think she's right when she says we should sell him on and get something more suitable."

I couldn't believe my ears. "You make it sound like we're shopping for a new pair of shoes! You can't just dump a horse because he's not *suitable*."

"I didn't say dump." Mum switched on the washer and glared back at me. "You made us buy him because you fell in love with the way he looks but now you know he's got all these faults—"

"He hasn't got faults!" I was starting to yell. "Problems—yeah, we've got problems, but nothing that can't be solved. If Raine would help instead of punishing us when things go a bit wrong—"

"You can't blame Raine," Mum said firmly. "She has to consider her other students *and* her horses. She told us you and Limelight are a potential danger to everyone, so I'm glad she's barred you from going out."

"Well, thanks a lot!" I shrieked and stamped out of the

laundry room before the tears prickling behind my eyes started to flow.

I slammed the door of my room and threw myself on the bed in an agony of self-pity. No one understood me; no one understood my beautiful, precious horse, and I hated them all. Gradually my sobs of rage subsided and I lay quietly hiccuping, thinking about the day I'd first seen Limelight. Mum was right about one thing: I truly had fallen instantly in love with him. His fine sleek lines, noble head, and stunning silver-gray color had swept me off my feet a hundred million times more than any great-looking movie star.

I'd wanted, longed for, *ached* for my own horse for four years while I'd learned to ride on the Marcus ponies, and had been deeply envious of Hannah when her folks bought sweet little Rafferty for her. I'd really started working on my own parents then, subjecting them to a constant barrage of please, please, *please*, until I'd worn them down and we'd gone horse-hunting a few weeks ago. We visited a few other ponies first, all recommended by Raine. Although they were nice I felt no spark, no connection, until I looked across the yard and saw Limelight, moving like a piece of equine poetry across his field. The owner wasn't sure about bringing him over. She said that although he was properly broken, the part-Arab needed schooling on and wasn't I a bit young? I've always been a bold rider, confident in my own abilities, and because I was so totally smitten I assured her he was perfect for me. The minute I approached Limelight and he dropped his soft velvet nose into my hand I knew there could be no other. Mum and Dad who know diddlysquat about horses were obviously doubtful but won over by the pony's sweet, affectionate nature.

"He's a lamb," the owner agreed. "But a handful to ride, so get plenty of help."

The trouble was I didn't want any help, not at first. I just wanted to enjoy my wonderful new boy, to revel in the glorious cadence of his stride and the heady excitement of his speed. It was only after I started losing control when he shied or bucked at something that startled him that help was something I very, very much needed. But now, as I sprawled miserably rubbing my sore, aching legs, I wondered if it was too late and I had let Limelight down by allowing bad habits to develop. Whatever happened, I swore to myself, I loved my horse and nothing and nobody was going to make me give him up.

Chapter Two

"Of course you're not going to give him up!" Hannah, like a true BFF, was 100 percent behind me. "I've been telling Molly about you and Limelight and there's loads you can do. Come round and meet her, Casey, she's totally mad but you'll like her."

Molly, I knew, was a visiting aunt, sister of Hannah's mother and a highly regarded artist, the creator of those weird but fabulous sculptures you see in magazines with names like *Homes of the Rich and Famous.*

"I can't muscle in on your family," I said into the phone. I'd stopped crying but still sounded pretty pathetic.

"Sure you can. Mum and Molly have been arguing all day so you'll make a good diversion."

A doubtful compliment but I could do with talking to someone with a positive take on Limelight, and the atmosphere in my home was definitely not encouraging. I hobbled the few blocks to Hannah's house. When the door was opened by an older version of my friend, someone with the same attractively gap-toothed grin and wild mop of hair, I knew this was Molly. She was *brilliant*. She listened intently to everything I told her, throwing in a couple of pertinent questions, then ran her fingers through her hair so it stood out like shock waves and looked right at me.

"Obviously the easiest thing would be to do what your folks and Raine have told you. Sell him to someone more experienced and get yourself something quieter, but I don't know about you, I don't like giving up on something worthwhile. If you love Limelight, and I can hear that you do, Casey, you're going to have to put in a heap of work."

"Anything, I'll do anything," I said eagerly.

"You keep him in a stall at the riding center, don't you?"

I nodded.

"That's the first change I'd make. Being confined does-n't suit his temperament, he's leaving his stable all fizzed up and full of energy. My guess is you've been letting him gallop when and where he likes—I'm right, huh?"

It was true. The excitement of having all that power and speed beneath me had clouded my judgment, and whenever we'd gone out I'd given him his head and let him run.

"Turn him out for a few days while your leg heals, catch him up every day obviously, lead him round, maybe even lunge him—but don't get on his back. Then saddle him up, take him in the school, and just walk and trot every day till he's convinced galloping is no longer part of his daily program. Every time he moves into a faster gait turn him in a circle till he comes back to walk or trot. He's only started running off with you the last week or two, so the habit's not deeply ingrained. A week or so should do it, still keeping him out at grass when he isn't working, still handling him as much as you can, and still keeping up the lunge lessons."

"I don't actually know how to lunge," I admitted. "And it sounds pretty dull. He likes excitement, so won't he get bored?"

"Get Raine to teach you lunging and no, with all that variety he won't get bored, but you might." Molly was pretty straight talking.

"It doesn't matter," I told her. "Like I said, I'll do *anything.*"

"Good for you." Her blue eyes crinkled in a smile. "I'd

get involved if I was going to be around—" She paused suddenly, then said, "Hey Hannah!"

"Uh-huh?" My friend gave the same warm smile.

"How about you and Casey staying at Forlorn over the summer vacation? There are acres of land and it's already fenced. I'm moving my palominos in as soon as the place is mine and I've already put *own horse welcome* on the student brochures. You can bring Rafferty and I'll get to meet Casey's Limelight."

"Wow! Hannah's eyes were shining as she turned to me. "Molly's buying Forlorn House out on the cape. It's the old family home where she and Mum grew up—Molly's going to run a summer school there for budding sculptors. Maybe we could get to come to the classes, too?"

Classes! Was she mad? We'd be staying with our horses on one of the most stunning bits of coast in the whole county, riding on the cliffs and the beach, maybe even in the ocean, and she wanted to join in some dumb art lessons?

"You won't want to do that, Hannah." Molly looked as amazed as I felt. "Your mum's always said one artist in the family is enough."

"Yeah, she told me that too, but I would *love* to learn."

My friend was practically jumping up and down. "So would Casey, I bet."

I composed my face into what I hoped was an enthusiastic expression. If getting a holiday with Limelight in a fantastic place with a knowledgeable, supportive person like Molly depended on a few dull hours slapping clay around, I was up for it.

"Oh yeah," I said. "It sounds terrific."

And that was it. Before Molly left, the arrangements were all made, including borrowing one of Raine's trailers for the horses and assuring my parents I'd be taking an already vastly improved Limelight with me. Raine was less easy to convince than they were, but after watching me patiently following Molly's instructions for Limelight's new regime, she started to come round and even agreed to show me how to lunge him. During the few weeks before our trip I felt the bond between my horse and me begin to strengthen. He was so much better for living out, Molly had been dead right about that, quickly shedding the pent-up frustration that had been making him increasingly wound up. Now his sweet nature came to the fore and he seemed to look forward to seeing me, cantering freely to the paddock gate as soon as he saw me arrive.

At first he tended to be over-boisterous, nudging me enthusiastically and dancing around while I put on his bridle, but gradually his manners improved. He learned to stand quietly while I checked him over and to walk out correctly, his beautiful head in line with my shoulder as he listened for any commands. To my surprise I really enjoyed those non-riding session the first few days. My leg and ankle were still pretty sore, but they improved with the gentle exercise and I loved the feeling of closeness that grew between Limelight and me during every fifteen-minute session. He was the sweetest pony, seeming to revel in having all my attention and trying to do everything I asked, rather like an affectionate if over-exuberant puppy. I was nervous he'd remember the last time I'd ridden him and simply bomb off as soon as I climbed into the saddle, but when—after three days—I rode him into the school, he set off obediently at walk. For once I concentrated on producing regular, unrestricted, and energetic strides rather than looking forward to upping the pace to canter as I usually did. My horse had a wonderfully natural free walk, a cool, loose sashay that needed no playing around with.

He was less impressive at trot, so I worked hard at getting more active hind legs and flexing hocks so that he pushed from behind rather than pulling from the front. Again, because we were working on improving balance and building confidence, I kept the schooling sessions short and varied them with some gentle lunging, supervised by a still-cynical Raine. Limelight showed no sign of either boredom or a desire to belt madly round the arena. Sometimes when I took him back to his field, he would, after politely dropping his nose into my hand, move a few paces away then suddenly tear off across the grass, bucking and kicking in a show-off display of energy, but I knew he was just being a kid letting off steam so it only made me laugh.

Several times in the school he tried to break into canter when I asked him to extend his trot but, keeping to Molly's instructions, I turned him immediately, asking for a twenty- meter circle at the correct pace. He very quickly learned to obey. Okay, I know it doesn't compare to galloping across country with the wind in your face and sheer excitement making your heart sing, but it was good, bonding, and entirely necessary if I was going to sort out our problems and keep this gorgeous, beautiful pony of mine.

I really, truly couldn't wait for the day Hannah and I set off for our vacation at Cape Forlorn, and the fact that the day dawned cold and blustery with dark, threatening clouds did nothing to quash my enthusiasm. Raine had eventually been impressed by the work I'd put in with Limelight, and she did tell my parents—if slightly grudgingly—how much he'd improved.

"As long as you do everything Molly tells you and don't go galloping off a cliff or anything." My poor mum still couldn't understand why I loved riding so much and obviously wished I'd take up macramé or something instead. "And promise you won't go out on your own."

"I promise." I double-checked that I had everything Limelight needed and climbed into the car driven by Hannah's dad, Terry. "Don't worry; we're going to have a great time."

"Yeee-hah!" Hannah stuck her head out the window. "She'll be fine. We're going to have the best vacation ever!"

The weather, though, seemed to have ideas of its own. I'd been waiting with eager anticipation to see Cape Forlorn, picturing it bathed in brilliant light—the hot sun, beating down from a cerulean sky, making tinsel waves on the ocean and turning the fields and woods on the cliffs above to emerald and ruby. Instead, as the car and trailer chugged slowly up the steep, narrow road leading to Forlorn House we stared out at a slate-gray sea, bitterly tossing beneath dense black clouds while the wind shrieked and rain lashed the windscreen in spiteful torrents. Misshapen trees bent their heads against the gale, and as we crested the hill a forked stab of lightning seemed to split the sky in two, followed almost instantly by a clap of thunder that exploded above us, to roll and reverberate around the car. Hannah and I jumped and clutched each other like we were watching a scary movie. I saw her finger point shakily ahead.

"That's it—that's F-forlorn House!"

I guess it was beautiful, one of the oldest houses I'd ever seen, but at that moment, rearing out of the blackened landscape, its crooked chimney seeming almost to touch another dramatic prong of lightning, it looked more like Dracula's Castle on a bad night.

"Lovely," I gulped. "Oh, Han, I hope the horses are okay."

It was our first concern, obviously, to get Limelight and Rafferty out of their small trailer, and I leapt out of the car to open the big farm gate at the entrance to the house's yard. I was soaked in minutes, seconds even, and had to use all my strength to push the heavy gate shut against the force of the howling wind. More lightning and another roar of thunder crashed around me as I ran across to where the car had pulled up.

"Leave the ponies where they are." Terry had to yell above the noise of the storm. "Run straight for the house!"

Hannah hesitated but I could hear Limelight whinnying, a high-pitched frightened sound, and I knew I had to go to him. Swiftly I slid in the trailer's side door and stood by his shoulder, talking him down with soothing nonsense phrases.

"It's okay, baby, it's okay. I'm here now, it'll be all right."

Louder than ever, the crash of thunder drowned my words, and even in here the harsh brilliance of lightning threw Limelight's terrified expression into sharp relief. He was rocking up and down with small, shuddering movements, and sweat had broken out on his neck and shoulders. I held him close, soothing, stroking, and hoping desperately he wouldn't rear up and smack his head or try to kick his way out.

"Casey shouldn't be in there!" I heard Terry shout. "If the horse goes loopy he could kill her in a confined space like that."

Not very helpful but I wasn't going anywhere without Limelight, so I carefully undid his lead rope. There was no way I could keep him calm in here; he'd be safer outside as long as I could hold on to him. Besides, he was upsetting Rafferty, whose placid, bombproof nature was having no trouble with the storm itself, and I didn't want Hannah's beloved pony hurt either. The best way to unload the trailer was via the ramp at the back, but there was no time so I walked forward with the terrified Limelight close by my side, telling him to remember all the things he'd learned and hoping against hope he didn't barge through me. The step down from the side door was tricky, and I felt my foot slip on its flooded surface—but I made it and managed to grip the rope as my pony clattered full-tilt beside me. We were doing okay, and we'd have been fine if only the storm hadn't sent the biggest thunderclap yet, hurling from the sky like a hand grenade aimed directly at us. Limelight whinnied in terror and tried to flee from the sound, rearing up, up into the lightning-torn sky. The wet lead rope burned through my hands, tearing off the skin, but my fingers tightened round the very end before I half fell and was almost dragged across the wet stones of the yard.

"Whoa, boy, whoa. You're all right now." Silhouetted like some kind of superhero, a tall, lean figure reached up and grabbed the rope, bringing the frightened horse back to ground. "In here." He moved fast, and I stumbled beside him into a big, warm barn smelling of hay and straw. He was incredibly strong, still keeping the panicky Limelight under control as he snapped on a switch, flooding the place with light. "Close the doors, Casey. We'll leave the storm outside, and your boy will soon calm down."

He was right. Released from the noisy metal confines of the trailer and muffled from the sights and sounds outside, Limelight soon stopped trembling and walked to me, dropping his nose in my scraped palm in his signature gesture of affection.

"Wow!" I breathed deeply and pushed back the wet hair plastered across my face. "Thanks so much Mr.—er—?"

"Sean. I'm Sean." He was soaked too, but in his case it just accented great cheekbones and a body to die for.

He held out his hand and smiled, and while I remember wishing I was looking a whole, *whole* lot better, I got the strongest, zingiest feeling that I was about to start one *heck* of a vacation at Forlorn House!

Chapter Three

"What about Hannah's pony—Rafferty, isn't it?" Sean was looking at Limelight with an admiring gleam in his eyes.

I wondered hopefully if the gleam was, in fact, for me but didn't think I could get that lucky. "He seemed pretty calm, he's a different temperament altogether, but—"

"But it can't be nice stuck out there on his own. I'll go and get him." Sean was evidently a man of action.

I watched him move purposefully into the maelstrom outside while I, gingerly holding a handful of straw in my sore hand, rubbed the worst of the rain from my horse's back. I had another scrape at my hair, smoothing it down and hoping the sleek look suited me. Limelight jumped and shuddered when the barn door opened again, bringing with it the noise of howling wind and rain, but I held his nose comfortingly and smiled at the welcoming whicker he gave to greet his friend Rafferty. Hannah's pony was heavily streaked with rain and his bushy black mane glittered with a million droplets, but as usual he was taking the situation in his stride. He now walked toward us as if it was the most normal thing in the world meeting up in a strange barn in the middle of a terrible storm.

"He's a cool one," Sean tickled Rafferty's ears. "He wasn't bothered at all about being in the trailer but I thought I'd bring him in anyway."

"Limelight's pleased to see him." I watched the ponies touch noses. "Um—thanks for your help, Sean."

"No prob." He lolled against a straw bale. "Molly told us about Limelight being easily spooked so I thought you might need a hand. She couldn't do anything herself because of her ankle."

"Ankle?"

"Yeah, she broke it—didn't you know?"

I shook my head, and he raised his eyebrows. "It was a couple of days ago, just after we arrived, so I thought she'd have said."

"What happened?" I was trying not to be selfish and think, *What about her helping me with my pony?*

"Some weird old guy suddenly stepped out of the trees when she was riding back from the beach. She was on Ozzie, unfortunately, and you know what he's like—great horse but spooks at his own shadow—and this time he took Molly by surprise and she came off and fell awkwardly."

"Poor Molly." I felt genuine sympathy. "I didn't know she had—well—a problem horse too."

"Oh, Ozzie's a million times better than he was, she's done wonders with him."

"It sounds as though you've known her a long time."

"Since I was two or three." He gave a grin that could knock your socks off. "She used to live next door, she taught me and Toby—he's my brother—to ride practically before we could walk."

"I didn't realize." I was feeling very comfortable and natural in his company. "I thought you were one of her Artsy-Fartsy students."

His grin got even wider. "I'll have to tell Molly you said that. Toby and I *are* students actually. He wants to specialize in metal and found-objects assemblage at this summer school, while I'd like to concentrate on figurative sandstone and wood carving."

I blinked. Had I just called this gorgeous guy Artsy-Fartsy?

"Terrific," I said, too heartily. "I—um—I thought I'd do—er—clay."

"Clay's good," he said solemnly and laughed at my stricken face. "You don't *have* to do any of the classes, Casey. Molly would be totally cool with that."

"No, I want to." It was true—well, I did *now.* "I'll have plenty of time on my hands anyway seeing as Molly can't help with my riding."

"She talked to me about that. She'll be around to give advice, and if you can put up with me I'll be glad to lend a hand."

"I guess that'll be okay." What I actually felt like saying was, *You better believe it!* But you have to be cool, don't you, so I added, "If you've been riding since you were two you must have—what?—eight or ten years' experience."

"Cheeky!" He grinned again. "I'm sixteen, that's six months, two weeks, and four days older than you."

"Not that you're counting." I grinned back, wondering just how much Molly had told him about me.

"I saw a photo of your last birthday celebration." Sean realized an explanation was called for. "That's how I know the date."

"Oh God!" I covered my face in embarrassment. "It wasn't the one of me and Hannah dressed as fairies, was it? She promised she wouldn't show that to anyone!"

I'd been wearing a very skimpy pink tutu as a joke and as soon as I saw Sean's grin widen again, I knew that he'd seen me. Luckily, before my face could get any redder the barn door opened and Hannah, her dad, and Molly came in.

"Thanks for unloading Rafferty." My friend gave her placid pony a hug. "Dad made me wait till the storm calmed down."

"It's moving away already." Molly, leaning heavily on a stick, waved her free hand at the weather outside. "The sky's much lighter and the thunder's already just a rumble in the distance. Sorry you had such a dramatic welcome to Forlorn House, Casey."

"It's okay. Sean was a big help getting Limelight in here. My poor horse was really spooked and you understand what that's like."

"Oh, you've heard about Molly's accident on Ozzie?" Hannah patted her aunt's shoulder gently. "Having a pony like Rafferty makes it hard for me to believe Ozzie would shy at a paper bag blowing in the wind, but you know how hyped up that type of horse can get, don't you, Casey?"

"Paper—" Sean looked surprised. "Why d'you say that?"

"It was the only thing I could think spooked my horse," Molly said quickly. I knew by the way she avoided his eyes that she wasn't telling the truth.

I opened my mouth to say, *What about the creepy old man then?* but closed it again. There was a distinct atmosphere, a restraint between Terry and Molly, and I thought I should stay well out of it.

"It's just one more thing that's gone wrong since you moved in here." Hannah's dad sounded really uptight. "And I'm not sure about leaving these girls with you, Molly. What with the staff walking out, the business with your father's portrait, and now this fall that's laid you up—"

"I'm not laid up, I just can't ride, and I didn't tell you before because I knew you'd react like this." Molly shifted her weight uncomfortably. "You're making too much of it,

Terry: You're as bad as my sister. The picture was simply an accident, two new ladies are due to start work on Monday, and Sean and Toby will make sure the girls get help with their riding and don't go out alone. None of it means anything; you're just letting your imagination run away with you."

"Not me," Terry said. "You know how your sister feels about you buying this house, Molly, and these so-called accidents just underline what a foolhardy thing it was."

"Superstitious nonsense," Molly said irritably. "Listen, I think it's stopped raining. You and Casey can take the horses over to their paddock if you like, Hannah."

"Hm," my friend said as we led Rafferty and Limelight across the yard. "I think Molly was getting rid of us so she can have a real go at my dad, don't you?"

"Maybe." I really, *really* hoped we'd be staying. "What exactly is the problem then? You said your mum and Molly were arguing a lot, but I didn't realize it was about this house."

"My folks haven't told me the whole story. It's like Mum doesn't want me to know. They're dead against Molly coming back here but I kinda thought it was because of sad memories. Their father died when they were quite young—drowned in a boat accident off the cape."

"That's probably it, and they don't like to talk about it." I checked my horse, who was starting to caper a bit. "Steady, Limelight. Sean might know, he used to live next door to Molly, she taught him and his brother to ride and everything."

"He is seriously cute." Hannah gave me a wicked glance. "I hope his brother's nice too."

"I don't know what you mean." I tossed back my still-damp hair. "They're both going to do the sculpture classes apparently."

"Don't tell me—you've developed a sudden passionate interest in art, haven't you?" Hannah said teasingly. "Tell you what, though, your new boyfriend can certainly move, can't he?"

Sean had gone ahead, wanting to make sure the other horses had dealt with the storm okay, while we followed more slowly. He'd just vaulted over the gate into a big paddock and was running easily across the grass to a group of ponies at the far end. He sure was a nice sight, and for once I found myself taking less interest in the horses. They were a handsome bunch, though, two palominos, a racy-looking chestnut, and a big bay so dark he looked almost black.

"The palominos are Ozzie and Mac," Hannah told me. "Only I don't know which is which. Molly says Toby owns the chestnut so I guess the black one is Sean's."

"He's stunning." I couldn't help thinking how great we were going to look together, the tall, dark Sean on his wickedly handsome dark bay and blond me on beautiful silver-white Limelight.

"You're going all gooey." Hannah pretended to slap me. "Call out and ask your boyfriend if we should let our horses go straight away."

"Stop calling him that." I made Limelight stand properly as I undid the gate. "He's coming back and if he hears I'll kill you!"

Sean, walking rapidly toward us, was followed by the dark bay.

"Meet Rifka." He stopped a few yards away, and the big horse halted immediately. "They're all pretty good-natured so you let your two loose and we'll watch them settle in."

I could feel Limelight's eagerness to be off as he waited patiently for me to remove his head collar. As always, he touched my palm briefly before moving away, then skittishly pranced sideways, watching for Rifka's reaction. Suddenly they were both off, cantering freely, heads and tails high as they wheeled and circled across the sparkling wet grass. One of the palominos called to them, then he too plunged and spun across the field to join in the glorious fun, galloping with flying leg changes, amazing pirouettes, and even airs above the ground.

"Fantastic!" Sean was smiling ruefully as he watched the beautiful sight. "They move so much better without riders cramping their style, don't they?"

"Some do." Hannah pointed to Rafferty, head down, busily munching. "Mine has different priorities, I think."

"Just like Mac." Sean laughed and nodded to where the other palomino placidly continued grazing. "It takes all sorts, I guess."

He was right, and though I wouldn't say it to my best friend, I was very glad I had the Limelight sort with all its complications! We sat on the gate and watched the six horses for ages. The storm had completely blown itself out now, and the sun filtered through raggedy scraps of cloud scudding overhead. Once they'd finished showing off,

Limelight, Rifka, and Ozzie indulged in a serious bout of rolling and we laughed to see three sets of legs, silver, black, and gold, waving enthusiastically in the air. That done, they all settled down to their grazing, and the big paddock was a peaceful sight in the now bright afternoon light.

"What a difference from when we arrived." Hannah stretched luxuriously. "I thought I'd messed up big time talking my folks into letting us come here, but now it looks great."

"How come you had to work on them so hard?" I said, surprised.

She shrugged. "Mum and Molly fell out years ago over some big family thing, and at first Mum didn't want me staying here. I said we had to, 'coz Molly had already gotten your parents to agree, and Dad backed me up. He reckoned it was about time Mum and Molly got over their row—he wanted us all to come to Forlorn House, in fact. Mum wouldn't do that but in the end she agreed to let me."

"I wondered why you didn't know Sean." I nodded at him. "Seeing as he was a neighbor of Molly's for years."

"I had the same thought." He looked candidly at Hannah. "It seemed strange we never saw you visit—but hey, if this family stuff is private—"

"It's okay." My friend ran a hand through her wild hair. "I don't know the whole story myself so there's not much I can tell anyone, and it's probably not that interesting. I'm with Dad on this one—whatever went wrong, we should all just move on."

"Mm." Sean stared at the ground for a moment, then turned his dark gaze back to her. "I did think it was— odd—the way Molly described her riding accident, though."

"Oh yeah." I turned to Hannah. "She told you and your dad that Ozzie spooked at a paper bag, but Sean said what scared the horse was a weird old man appearing from behind a bush."

"It was—I should know because I was there. Toby and I wanted to see the beach the day we arrived, so Molly rode down with us. Oz freaked out on the way back." Sean looked uncomfortable. "But it's none of my business what Molly tells your dad, is it? So just forget what I said."

"Don't worry about upsetting me," Hannah laughed, "Casey'll tell you I'm like Rafferty, it takes hell of a lot to rattle me, so you don't have to tiptoe around."

"Adults say strange stuff all the time," I said, laughing with her. "So there's no point in making a big deal out of Molly's little white lie. The weird old man will probably never be seen again, so why worry?"

With hindsight I have to say it wasn't the best prediction I've ever made, but how was I to know the big, *big* trouble that was waiting to happen on Cape Forlorn?

Chapter Four

To start with, though, it was one big laugh. Returning to the house, we heard the roar of a motorbike. Sean said, "Here comes my brother. Brace yourselves!"

I didn't understand what he meant till six feet of leather-clad eighteen-year-old bounced into the room.

"You've arrived! Sorry I wasn't here—didn't fancy getting struck by lightning, so I sheltered in town. You've gotta be Hannah—just like your aunty!" He grabbed my friend and gave her a bear hug, then turned to me. "Good on you, Sean, mate, I leave you for a couple of hours and you've got *two* gorgeous girls in tow. Hiyah, I'm Toby."

"Um, Casey," I said and found myself enveloped in a powerful leather embrace.

"Nice to meet you, Casey." He grinned and looked around. "And where's my favorite gal?"

"And that would be—?" Molly limped in, leaned against

a table, and waggled her stick threateningly at him. "Don't you dare pick me up and cuddle me again, Toby Marsh, or I'll clout you with this."

"You know you love me really." Toby zipped himself out of his biking gear. "I'm starving. Oh hi, you must be Hannah's dad, Terry isn't it?"

I was quite sorry he only shook hands, thinking a swift hug might loosen up Terry's rigid-looking back.

"Mrs. Fellows said to tell you supper will be ready in ten minutes," he said. "Are you girls okay? Horses settled in?"

"Yes and yes. Relax, Dad, it's brilliant here, we're going to have a great vacation."

Terry tried to look convinced and cheered up a lot when we started on the excellent food Molly's housekeeper had cooked. Anyway we were all discovering it was impossible to be in Toby's company and not laugh. The two brothers were similar looking, though I preferred Sean's, dark smoldering style to Toby's extrovert exuberance. Toby couldn't wait to meet the students, due to arrive the next morning.

"Two more lovely girls," he said,, rubbing his hands together. "Both eighteen, I think you said, Molly."

"I did." She pretended to be stern but smiled at him indulgently. "And I also said the other two are nineteen-year-old guys, so cool it, chum."

"Nah, bit of competition never hurt anyone. Me and Sean will be the welcoming party if you like."

"You won't get time. You promised to help Mrs. Fellows clear up after breakfast."

"So I did. I can't believe those two local morons walked out on you because of some old ghost story." He didn't notice the sharp look Molly shot him, but I did. "When does the new help arrive?"

"Monday," Sean said repressively, watching Terry's reaction. "So we only have one day of lending a hand. It won't kill us."

"What's this about a ghost—?" Terry began.

Molly's shoulders tensed with irritation. "It was just an excuse, they found Forlorn House too remote, decided to work in Headley instead."

"Are you sure—?" Terry started again.

Hannah, desperate to stop him finding a reason to make us leave, said recklessly, "Yeah, Dad, definitely. Sean heard them say so, there's no problem."

Sean looked understandably surprised seeing as he'd said no such thing, but quickly caught on and backed her up, managing to change the subject at the same time. "That's right. Say, Terry, Hannah tells me you're an engineer—could you take a look at my brother's motorbike, d'you think?"

"I'm not a mechanic, but it's a Harley, isn't it?" His eyes gleamed, "I'm a bit of a fan so I wouldn't mind a look. What exactly's wrong?"

"Noth—" Toby got a heavy nudge from Sean. "I mean, it's just I'm not sure if it's running totally smoothly. Maybe you could listen to the engine."

They were a pretty smart pair, the way they'd understood the situation, I thought, and I smiled when I saw Molly surreptitiously pat Sean on the back. While the three of them went out to worship the Harley, Hannah and I helped clear the table and stack the dishwasher.

"Luckily the students' rooms are all ready," Molly told us. "So there won't be too many chores tomorrow, but I'd appreciate a hand."

"Sure thing," Hannah said. "I'll help get a really early breakfast ready if you like."

"Why?" Her aunt looked bemused.

"So we can get rid of Dad as soon as possible! He's doing my head in, being all negative about us staying here."

"He's worrying in case anything else goes wrong and your mum can say to us both *I told you so.*" Molly smiled ruefully. "I should have told them about my ankle and the other problems but I really wanted you here, it's about time I got to know you."

"And we want to be here, don't we, Casey?"

I nodded enthusiastically but found myself wondering about all the strange things that seemed to have happened since Molly came back to Forlorn House. I just hoped she was right and there was no connection between the story of the ghost, the broken portrait, and the spooky old man who'd caused her accident. Terry, having enjoyed his inspection of Toby's motorbike, now seemed inclined to believe Molly had simply had a run of bad luck, and shortly after breakfast the next day he drove off, leaving a highly relieved Hannah and me to start our summer. The weather, too, seemed to have decided to cooperate, and the woods and fields surrounding the house lay bathed in sunshine.

"Gorgeous!" Hannah flopped down in the shade next to

her bay pony. "Rafferty's found a nice cool spot, haven't you, babe? Hey, how far away is the beach? Could we ride there before the students arrive?"

"Yeah, it's only twenty minutes or so." Sean saw me bite my lip nervously. "It's a twisting old track, so we mostly walk it."

"Right." I took a deep breath. "I haven't ridden Limelight out since he ran off with me weeks ago, but I'm sure we'll be fine."

"Keep behind me and Rifka," Sean said quietly. "We'll keep the pace down so your horse won't get over-excited and want to tank off. He can burn up his energy with a nice cool swim."

"In the ocean?" I was thrilled at the thought.

"No, in your bathtub—where d'you think?" The irrepressible Toby was already leading Khan across the field. "Come on, you guys, last one to saddle up gets the ugliest student."

"Charming, isn't he?" Sean winked at me. "Personally I couldn't care less if they all turn out to look like movie stars—I'm more than happy with the company I've got."

I felt myself coloring up and buried my face in Limelight's silky mane, pretending to fiddle with his lead rope. Despite all their rolling, the horses only needed a quick brush. We were soon riding out of the yard gate, where a wistful-looking Molly waved us good-bye. She'd got the blacksmith to remove Mac and Ozzie's shoes so the palominos could enjoy a few weeks' rest while her ankle mended, but I knew she was longing to join us. She'd already been through Limelight's routine with me, pleased the schooling was working so well, and now assured me a quiet hack to the beach was no problem.

"Don't do any galloping at all," she instructed. "You can build up to that with Sean's help. He's not only a terrific rider, he's a true horseman in my opinion, so trust him and go by what he tells you. Oh, and Casey—"

I turned to look at her.

"Have a fabulous time!"

I was so looking forward to my first ocean trip on horseback, I had every intention of doing just that. The scenery on the cape was stunning, rolling grandly into the distance, but I knew how bleak it could look in different weather conditions. The track we were using was, as Sean told me, narrow and winding, its coarse sand peppered with stones, so we had the horses pick their way carefully along it at walk. Broad-leaved, stubby grass grew in patches and after a while we trotted through these, with Limelight starting to pull a little. Sean kept Rifka firmly ahead, the big dark bay's calm presence soothing Limelight so I could relax and feel him come back to my hands.

"That's better." Sean turned and gave me that knee-melting grin. "You two are doing fine. Five more minutes and we'll be clambering down a cliff—can you smell the sea?"

An exhilarating salty tang was indeed in the air. I held my breath as we crested a hill and there, spread below us, was the ocean in all its sparkling glory. All four horses caught the excitement, whinnying and stamping their hooves, and I was pleased when Limelight listened to my voice and obeyed hands and legs to quiet down.

"The path down is pretty gentle; use a loose rein and have your weight back in the saddle," Sean said. Remembering Molly's words, my horse and I followed him trustingly over the cliff.

Well, not right over, obviously, but it felt a bit like that despite his description of the "gentle" path. There was no need to worry about Limelight rushing it or playing up, he was concentrating too hard and I was very proud of him when he reached the foot of the steep cliff and took his first steps on the beach. The sand, as on all the other coves on Cape Forlorn, was fine, golden, and inviting, but unlike most it was completely deserted.

"The cliff's too steep for the tourists," Sean explained. "So Molly tells us we'll nearly always get it to ourselves."

I was glad about that, being wary of the chaos Limelight might inflict a crowd of unsuspecting sunbathers! Again, Sean led the way, taking us to the damp, firm sand at the very edge of the ocean. The sea lapped peacefully against our horses' legs, its clear turquoise blue edged with frothy white lace. Rifka was keen to go deeper and strode out confidently. Soon the gentle waves swirled around his knees while he bent to sniff the water curiously. Rafferty and Khan followed him but Limelight seemed to want to stay at the edge of the shallows, keeping in line with the others as they moved along the curving line of the bay.

"Come and join us, Casey." Hannah was enjoying herself. "We're not going to swim yet, just paddle till they get the feel of it."

"Limelight's not sure; I'll let him do it in his own time."
I could feel my pony's resistance to moving into deeper
water, though he responded readily when I asked for trot,
then canter on the damp sand. Sean, Hannah, and Toby
were cantering too, their horses surging through the waves,
sending a million shining drops skyward as they splashed
and plunged. Limelight seemed to enjoy the sensation of
moving through the frothing edge of the water, but every
time I urged him farther in to join his friends he resisted
stubbornly. Hannah was having much more success: After
fooling around knee-deep for a while she was pleading to
swim.

"Rafferty just loves the sea!" She turned the bay pony
beachward. "I'm going to leave his saddle on those rocks,
strip off, and see how far we'll go!"

"I'll stay with you, Casey." Sean's dark eyes were sympathetic. "Not all horses take to the ocean straight away.
We've got all summer to persuade Limelight to try."

"He doesn't seem scared—just reluctant." It was really
bugging me. "Maybe he'll take a lead from you if I stay
close."

"He'll probably follow Rafferty." Toby had already taken

off Khan's saddle and was climbing out of his boots and jeans. "Sean can lead, then you go close behind Hannah. I'll bring up the rear so Limelight doesn't duck out."

"Okay, thanks." I was just dying to feel the sensation of my horse swimming.

We stacked the saddles on a rock that we used to climb back aboard. Rifka was mad keen to get back in the water, and Sean, looking drop-dead gorgeous in just a pair of shorts, had to work hard to keep him at walk. Rafferty too was all eagerness, little ears pricked forward as he followed the big dark bay into the water. Limelight went forward all right, but despite using my legs like never before, he just wouldn't budge beyond the sea's edge.

"Come on, Limelight, your mate's leaving you!" Toby pointed to where Rafferty was surging through the waves. I thought the idea was that we stayed close behind and felt annoyed with Hannah that she'd swarmed off like that. She turned and saw us and steadied the bay pony immediately.

"Sorry, I thought you were with us. I'll come back, shall I?"

I could see she and her horse were only a minute away from their first-ever swim.

"No, you go on," I called back. "I'll keep trying."

Limelight, all four hooves planted firmly on the sand, had other ideas, refusing point-blank to shift. Sean, looking like some kind of sea god, was now cresting the waves as Rifka swam effortlessly through the deeper water. Rafferty, fat and shining as a seal pup, was swimming too, making Hannah laugh for the sheer joy of it.

"I'll come and help," Sean yelled, turning his horse's head toward us.

"Nah, don't worry, bro, I'll *tow* the silver devil in!" Toby urged Khan alongside us and took a tight grip on Limelight's rein. "Kick him on, Casey; let's get this show on the road—or at least on the ocean!"

Taken by surprise, Limelight took several paces forward, moving deeper into the sea, but just as I thought my swimming dream was about to be realized, the naughty pony stopped dead and jerked his head back hard. Poor Toby, bareback on an already wet and slippery Khan, had no chance, sliding straight off his horse to land spread-eagled on the seafloor with its gentle waves washing right over him. To my relief he scrambled immediately to his feet, spluttering a lot and calling Limelight the rudest names I'd ever heard.

Sean, trying not to laugh, called out, "Don't worry, I'll catch your horse," because Khan of course had simply swum out to join him.

Limelight, who'd never before performed a really good rein-back, now decided that taking several steps backward in a straight line was the easiest thing in the world, and despite my efforts to stop him we were soon on the dry sand again.

"Sorry, Toby." I felt such an idiot. "You go and have your swim."

He waved a hand and took off through the water to meet up with his brother, who was still cutting easily through the ocean on Rifka with Khan swimming beside them. Toby slid onto his horse's back, and I watched enviously as the three riders enjoyed the (no-doubt) brilliant sensation of their horses swimming. I schooled Limelight on the sand, making him work hard at perfecting his trot–canter transitions while maintaining balance and rhythm. Yeah, dead boring, but I knew I had to reestablish my authority—Limelight had disobeyed big time, so obviously a lot more work needed doing.

I tried hard not to be resentful of the others when they came back to shore and dried off after their great time. They'd tried to help but I knew the responsibility of getting my pony and me on track lay firmly at my door, and despite this setback I was still determined to get it right.

Chapter Five

Because we'd stayed longer on the beach than we intended we were late getting back to Forlorn House.

"We'll be in trouble," Sean warned his brother. "We promised Molly we'd help welcome the students. With her ankle she can't show them round the house or anything."

"You've still got five minutes," I said, checking my watch. "If you run you can be at the gate when their taxi arrives."

"What about our horses?" Sean turned those wonderful melting eyes on me.

"Just leave them," I said. "I'll take care of them."

"You're a star, Casey!" Toby leapt off Khan, handed me his reins, and was gone.

"He can sort the students on his own." Sean started taking Rifka's saddle off.

"No he can't—Molly wants you both there." Hannah

gave him a shove. "Go on, I'll give Casey a hand."

She and I untacked the horses, washed the sea salt off, returned them to their field, and were walking back to the house before Sean came running toward us.

Hannah smiled and said sweetly under her breath, "Mm, funny how he's looking just at you. It's like I've become invisible—you would tell me if that's happened, wouldn't you, Case?"

I nudged her to shut up. "Hiyah, Sean. Rifka's fine, you can check if you want."

"No, I trust you." He walked very close. "Thanks a lot. As it happened only the two girls showed up—the guys aren't due for another hour so Toby could have managed. He's in his element, showing Heather and Sandy round the place. They haven't stopped giggling yet."

"He does do a great clown act," I said. "What are they like—the two girls, I mean?"

He shrugged. "Okay, seemed nice enough. One's very tall; the other's tiny so my brother's already calling them the long and the short."

"Have they brought horses?" Hannah asked.

"No. They're passionate about the sculpture classes;

want to concentrate on that with just a bit of walking and sunbathing."

I'd practically forgotten about the arty side of our stay, having neglected to look at the studio when Molly showed it to Hannah, so I thought I ought to manufacture a bit of interest. Sean took me round the big, airy room, which, instead of being the bohemian mess of paint and clay I'd envisaged, was scrupulously tidy and well organized. Underneath benches lining the walls were deep drawers holding a bewildering (to me) array of things from brass brazing rods, tins of laminating resin, powder pigments, and rolls of jute to some seriously fearsome-looking tools including an arc welding unit, clamps, saws, chisels, hammers, and awls. Sean told me what they all were but I didn't have a clue what you *did* with them, hoping Molly would soon enlighten me.

"Presumably you and all the other students have done some of this before." I indicated the charts and illustrations pinned on the walls. "Hannah and I haven't done anything except a bit of pottery at school. And even then everyone thought my ceramic pot was some kind of deformed cat."

He laughed. "Don't worry. Molly thought you two

would just be doing vacation stuff—swimming and riding and exploring the cape—so she won't be expecting you to know anything. Toby's the talented one in our family, but Molly, who got us both started a few years back, says my wood carving is worth developing."

"As long as none of you holds my ignorance against me—oh, you must be Heather, or are you Sandy?"

A very tall, thin girl had come in so quietly, I hadn't heard her. "Heather. Hi. I just wanted another look at the studio. Isn't it wonderful?" She waved long-fingered hands expressively.

"Yes," I said, being very positive. "Absolutely. Are you settled in okay?"

"Haven't unpacked yet. Sandy's getting Toby to help her, and I felt like a spare part."

I saw the quick grin that crossed Sean's face and said hurriedly, "We'll show you round outside if you want. We've got horses—"

"Oh, I don't do horses." She gave an exaggerated shudder. "Though I do find their form very pleasing in an artistic sense."

I couldn't think what to say to that and was glad when

Toby and a still-giggling Sandy appeared.

"Toby said he'll take us to the beach after lunch." Sandy was tiny with pretty, doll-like features.

"Not me, thanks," Heather said. "I want to sit outside and breathe in the atmosphere, maybe make a sketch or two."

I wondered if they were all going to be this arty, thinking if so I'd spend even more time with my horse than I'd planned.

"You'll come, won't you, Sean?" Toby seemed slightly alarmed at the thought of doing the beach trip with just Sandy.

"Only if Case—if the girls do."

"We've got to wait and see the other two students arrive," I said. "But you don't have to stay—we'll be fine."

"No, I want to help. Molly's up against it till the new staff get here. Looks like just you and—er—Sandy, bro."

Sean grinned at Toby's expression, and I had to fight down a laugh myself. Hannah, busy in the kitchen, didn't know why we were so amused.

"Sandy's already showing all the signs of having a crush on Toby." I double-checked to make sure the two girls couldn't hear. "It's his own fault, the way he flirts and jokes around."

"Yeah, he's nothing like his brother, who I notice still only has eyes for you." Hannah pretended to be upset. "All this romance—you're all so wrapped up in it, no one has time for poor little me!"

"Okay, right, so you might as well just stay in here and do all the chores while we get all the fun." I picked up some knives and forks. "Shall I set the table for lunch?"

"Please." She was cutting lovely-smelling crusty bread. "It's salad stuff—Mrs. Fellows is cooking properly tonight when we're all here."

The meal was fine except for Heather asking Molly a different sculpture question with every bite.

"Let's wait till classes start tomorrow, shall we?" Molly looked a bit dazed. "Just relax today and get to know one another. Paul and—um—Mikey will be here in a couple of hours."

In fact it was nearly three by the time the taxi from nearby Headley came chugging up the hill. Hannah, Sean, and I were lolling around in the yard, all indoor chores done, waiting to be a welcoming party. Toby and Sandy were at the beach and Heather, still chuntering about form, color, and shape to anyone who'd listen, was on a hammock seat at the back of the house, taking in the glorious view. Paul got out of the car first, tallish, fairish, and slightly serious, followed by a shorter guy with a cheeky grin who bounced over and said, "Hi, I'm Mikey, glad to meet you."

Hannah and I tried to help with their bags but they wouldn't let us, so we took them inside to meet Molly who was resting her ankle on a fat, embroidered stool. Paul was obviously pretty much in awe of the renowned sculptor but, unlike Heather, didn't go on and on. Mikey seemed more interested in the house, exclaiming at its age and being highly impressed it had been the Renshaw family home in former times.

"It wasn't as big then, of course," Molly explained. "When we left—oh, twenty-five years ago—it was extended and turned into a small hotel. Your rooms are in the new part, not so much history but better plumbing."

Mikey also seemed taken by the similarity in Molly and Hannah's looks.

"Amazing." He very gently touched my friend's wild hair. "You probably look exactly the same as your aunty did when she was your age."

"Mm." Hannah didn't seem to mind his close scrutiny, and if I didn't know her so well I'd swear she was batting her eyelashes. "There's a picture of Molly winning a cup at a horse show over there. She must have been about fifteen."

Mikey picked up the framed photo and squinted at it. "Spitting image! And you ride too, don't you?"

Hannah told him about Rafferty, adding, "We were hoping some of you might have brought your horses along."

"Never been on one. I'm a city boy but I'd love to try."

Molly's idea of us all getting to know each other seemed to be working, with me and Sean getting on like a house on fire, Toby and Sandy at the beach, and now Mikey arranging his first-ever riding lesson with Hannah. It only needed the quiet Paul to sweep Heather off her feet and we'd all be sorted! The meal was great with gorgeous food and everyone in high spirits. There was a lot of arty talk round the table, sculpting techniques and exhibitions visited, but I noticed Hannah and Mikey were deep in conversation about horses while Sean wanted to know how I felt about Limelight's performance on the beach.

"I was totally fed up at not swimming with him," I admitted. "It was frustrating not being able to get him into the sea."

"Yeah, it was a real pain for you," he agreed. "But I was kinda glad at the way he reacted."

"Glad?" I stopped shoveling in the delicious supper and looked at him. "Why?"

"When Molly told me about Limelight running off with you, I was worried you had a real problem on your hands. Once a horse has established bolting away as an answer to any situation he doesn't like, it's a very difficult habit to break. And it's such a dangerous thing for him to do—well, your experience must have shown you that."

"Terrifying," I said with feeling. "It's true Limelight didn't try tanking off with me today but I don't see how refusing to budge is such a good thing!"

"It's not, but it's a lot easier to work on. The actual problem you have is that Limelight doesn't completely trust you. Horses are herd animals—they need a leader to tell them when it's okay for them to do something, and Limelight, being a very high-spirited type, is challenging you."

"So that's why he didn't listen when I tried to stop him bolting?"

He nodded. "There was probably a reason he started running, and then of course he got himself on a speed high. The good thing is you seem to have made great headway on that one by taking galloping out of his agenda, though of course you'll want to reintroduce it on your terms."

"Oh yeah, I'd hate not being able to gallop cross-country ever again—but only when I know I'm in control."

"You'll definitely get to that point." He gave me that devastating smile. "And I'd like to help—but only if you want me to."

"Sure," I said casually, thinking, *Of course I do!*

After we'd eaten and Hannah, Sean, and I had helped with the clearing away, we followed Hannah into a pretty, cozy room we hadn't seen before.

"This is Molly's private study," she told us. "She said I could bring you in and show you a photo of my grandfather."

"Is this the picture that got broken in the move?" I asked.

"Yeah, one of the removal men dropped it when he brought it in. The two local women who were working here made a big deal about it being a weird thing to happen and a bad omen, but Molly says it was just a straightforward accident. She's going to have new glass made before she hangs it up properly."

The big photo was on the mantelpiece, propped against the wall. The frame was dented and the shattered glass had been removed, but it was a good picture of the subject. Hannah's granddad—Molly's father, of course—was at the wheel of a boat, smiling directly at the camera. His short, dark hair was tousled; his teeth very white, his eyes very blue, and he looked relaxed and happy.

"It's hard to tell if there's a family likeness." I peered closer. "I think his eyes are the same blue as yours and Molly's, but it's difficult to see the rest of his features."

"Yeah, we don't have a full beard like he did!" Hannah ran a finger over the smiling face. "His name was Andrew Renshaw and he looks nice. I wish I'd known him but my mum's five years younger than Molly, so she was only ten when he died. She doesn't seem to have many memories of her dad."

"It was a boat accident, wasn't it?" Sean asked gently. "I know the seas around the cape can get pretty fearsome in a storm."

I pictured the ocean the way it looked when we arrived, lashed by wind and rain into a dark, churning maelstrom of towering waves and vicious currents.

"I'd hate to be out in a boat in weather like that." I shivered at the thought. "It must be the spookiest—"

A scream, high-pitched with genuine terror, cut through my words, and all three of us jumped, startled.

"It came from the TV room." Sean was already running toward the hall. "Come on—quick!"

Hannah and I raced after him, clutching each other's hand for comfort. The big room with its squashy sofas and chairs was lit only by the flickering screen of the TV; beyond that, still staring wildly into the darkness outside the window, was Sandy. Sean ran to her and she threw herself against him, plucking at his sleeve in agitation.

"Out there—out there—something—someone—a ghost!"

Molly, limping as fast as she could, arrived at the door. "It's all right, Sandy, calm down. Now, what exactly did you see, dear?"

"I saw a—a movement, something hovering pale against

66

the window. He—he seemed to be looking in but—but I couldn't tell because he was wearing a hooded thing and I could only see his eyes—dead, staring eyes—because of his beard, a big full beard covering half his face."

I felt a sudden chill, as though ice water was running down my spine, and tried not to think of the photo we'd just been examining—the picture of Hannah's full-bearded *long-dead* grandfather!

Chapter Six

Luckily, before I could open my mouth and blurt out something stupid, Sean disentangled himself from Sandy's grasp and said, "That sounds like the old guy the other day, doesn't it, Molly?"

I saw Molly stiffen. "Old guy?"

"The one who was lurking about in the grounds. The one who spooked Ozzie."

"What imaginations you've all got!" Her smile was definitely strained. "Ozzie flipped at some paper blowing around, hardly noticed that old fella."

"What was the man doing around Forlorn House anyway?" Hannah wanted to know. "And why's he still outside scaring Sandy like that?"

"I'm sure Sandy just caught the reflection of the TV screen in the windowpane," Molly said firmly. "The old chap the other day had simply lost his way—he wouldn't be here at this time of night."

"I'll go out and check." Sean sounded pretty tough, but I was glad when he yelled upstairs for Toby to go with him.

The brothers took torches before going outside; although only evening, it was very dark in this isolated, unlit spot. Sandy, who now seemed to be enjoying the attention, was relating the story to Mikey, Hannah, and Paul, who'd missed the whole thing.

"You can't hear anything that goes on in this part of the house once you're upstairs in the newer bit," Mikey complained. "I'd have gone on the ghost hunt with the other guys if I'd known."

"Don't you start—there *is* no ghost hunt," Molly snapped. "The trouble is you're all used to the city—things look different out here with no street- or shop lights, so I hope you're not going to spook at every little thing."

She limped out of the room and we heard her checking with Sean and Toby. "Nothing out there? No—I told you so!"

"*Thanks for checking* would be nice," Toby muttered as he came in to join us. "What's bugging Molly? She's usually such a cool lady—who's making her so mad?"

"Me I suppose," Sandy said, reverting to her little-girl-lost act. "But I was really, really scared, Toby." She moved in close, but he ducked neatly out of her way. "I was sure there was someone outside looking in at me."

"Nope." He kept his voice very upbeat. "I promise we had a good look round so you don't have to worry. How about a game of something, everyone—I reckon the mood could do with a little lifting here."

He was right, we were all a bit subdued—mostly by Molly's vehement denial that anything was wrong—but once we got playing his silly, raucous game we quickly got back to normal. I wondered if our sleep would be shattered by any more "ghost sightings," but the night passed perfectly peacefully. When we came down to breakfast Mrs. Fellows was being helped by two capable-looking women who came, she told us, from an agency the other side of Headley. Neither of them seemed troubled by the possibility of Forlorn House being haunted, and I told myself firmly they were right.

After checking on the horses, Sean and I scrubbed our hands well and made our way to the studio for Molly's introductory lesson. She was a little pale, I thought, but had regained her cheerful composure and her "welcome to sculpture school" was really interesting. I'd been right—everyone else had previous experience in at least one of the techniques we were going to be shown. Two of the students, Heather and Mikey, had actually won scholarships to highly regarded art colleges.

Molly said it didn't matter how much or how little we knew. "This summer school is to show even an experienced sculptor the possibilities of materials and techniques. We can start with a medium of your own choice, then expand and extend as the course progresses. If there are specifics you need to know, that's what I'm here for. From my point of view, I'd like to see your expression and creativity grow as well as the hands-on crafting."

My hands-on crafting, I thought dismally, didn't have much to do with either expression or creativity, but I'd said I'd give it a go. I listened carefully on how to get started, choosing to do some drawings rather than making a maquette (a small, scaled-down version of the finished article). Everyone else already had a subject in mind. Sean was to work on a wood carving of a rearing horse, Sandy the cast of a mythical sea creature, Paul a Native American head carved from an aerated concrete block, Toby an abstract, Mikey a metallic figure, and Hannah a simplistic plaster bird. Heather, to my surprise, had also chosen a horse.

"I made loads of sketches yesterday and I really like this one of Toby's horse. He was scratching his ear with his hind foot—I didn't know they did that but it makes the most divine shape, which I'd like to sculpt in clay."

"They all sound good." Molly turned to me. "Any ideas, Casey?"

"Um," I said, trying to visualize something easy. "A tree."

She nodded. "Any particular kind?"

"I don't know the name but one of those we saw when we turned onto the coast road of the cape. The wind was blowing a gale and the tree was all bent and misshapen."

"Excellent. Start with a drawing, then I'll explain its limitations."

"Limitations?" I whispered to Sean.

"It's two-dimensional, for a start, so you can't produce an equivalent. Molly will show you how to make an armature."

He might as well have been talking a foreign language. Still, I listened and watched and actually quite enjoyed my first morning as a budding sculptor despite only having a few shaky sketches and the beginnings of a wood-and-aluminum frame on which my armature (which, I was told, is the sort of skeleton of the sculpture) would be built. I was glad to get back in the fresh air outside after lunch, though. Classes were scheduled for mornings only, which left the rest of the day for sun and sea and *riding*.

Mikey was dead keen to have his first experience of equitation, and we headed off for the corner of another field that Molly had earmarked for a sand school. She'd only got as far as fencing an area of twenty by sixty meters, but there was a good, cushioning cover of grass, markers, and even some colored poles. Hannah, who'd spent a lot of time explaining theory, she told me, wasted no time in getting Mikey into Rafferty's saddle. The patient bay pony stood like a rock, despite some ungainly flailing and heaving by the not very tall Mikey, and set off obediently at the walk as soon as Hannah instructed him. Sean had very kindly volunteered to help with my warm-up and lateral routine, and he made me work hard for thirty minutes or so.

"Great. I can see the partnership taking shape." He looked up at me. "And shape is what we're aiming for."

"Especially Heather and her sculpture, but I bet Lime-light makes a far better 'model horse' than she can."

"Could be." He laughed and patted my pony's gleaming shoulder. "Shall we take your boy out for a trial spin, then? Just a few canters, nothing too explosive."

"Sure." There was still a niggling fear in my brain. "Are you coming, Han?"

"No, we'll carry on here, and Rafferty will have earned a rest after that. Mikey thought we might go down for a swim later."

This meant walking to a gently sloping beach south of the house rather than the one with steep cliffs to the north.

"We can't take the horses there, it'll be full of tourists," Sean said. "I thought we could explore farther up the Cape instead."

"Fine by me." I stamped down the nervous, jittery feeling. "See you later, guys."

Hannah and Mikey hardly noticed us leave, absorbed as they were in his riding lesson. "They're getting on well," I remarked as we made our way back to the paddock for Rifka. "Considering Mikey's quite a bit older than Han."

"Yeah, but he seems a young nineteen and a real nice

guy. He's dead keen on learning to ride too."

"That *must* make him all right then," I teased. "I don't think you should trust people who put art above horses!"

We left Forlorn House's grounds at a quiet medium walk, following the narrow track that led to the steep cliffs. There was no one else around—no surprise, as I knew that the two girls had gone into Headley and Toby was giving Paul a spin out on the Harley.

"We're exploring today so we won't go down to the beach." Sean turned in his saddle to look at me. "That okay?"

"Yep." I was relieved I wasn't going to embarrass myself again trying to get Limelight into the sea, but still apprehensive about his tanking off. Once we'd got beyond the horses' beach and left the cliff edge, the track widened into a curving sweep of close-packed turf, perfect for galloping. I saw Rifka bounce excitedly and felt my fingers clamp tightly round the reins. This immediately sent Limelight into the high-strung jogging pace I hated. Expecting him to take off, I tensed even further.

"Whoa, relax." Sean brought Rifka back to a smooth walk. "*Relax*, Casey, and don't hang on to him so tight."

"If I let go he'll bolt," I said between gritted teeth.

"No, if you soften your hands you'll relieve the pressure that's winding him up. There's nothing here to spook him, and by relaxing you're telling him everything's fine."

I took a deep breath and did as he said, softening hands and body to sit lightly with a gentle, steady contact on the bit. The difference was amazing: My pony stopped dancing, dropped his nose, and walked out perfectly.

"Good one." Sean winked at me. "We're going to canter up that hill ahead, a nice working pace, no racing. If you feel Limelight trying to break away, turn him in a circle. There's plenty of room."

I hadn't realized how much being run away with had scared me—my mouth was dry and dusty with terror—but I nodded and concentrated on staying relaxed and in control. Limelight was a bit over-eager to begin with, but when I wouldn't let him race alongside Rifka he again accepted the bit and stayed behind the dark bay. When we pulled up at the top of the hill you'd think I'd just won first prize in some sort of competition, I was so thrilled. Sean didn't make a big deal of it, just flashed me one of his great smiles and pointed to our left.

"That wood looks interesting, and it'll be nice and cool. Shall we take a look?"

It was fantastic up here on the wilder end of the cape, with stunning views of the sea on our right shoulder and acres of countryside to be explored on our left. The wood was cool and shady, its rustling canopy of green leaves filtering the afternoon sun. We rode silently for a while, enjoying the tranquility, then Sean suddenly hopped off and started lugging a fallen branch around.

"If I stack a few of these into a mini jumping course we can pop the horses over."

Again my first reaction was of fear: Limelight might get over-excited and start running—look how he'd bombed through the trees last time—but I was determined not to be a sap. It was great of Sean to put up with this steady, cautious pace instead of cantering and galloping around, as I was sure he usually did.

"Okay." I drew my stirrups up a couple of notches. "You go first then."

He vaulted back in the saddle and turned his horse away from the logs.

"Tuck in behind me if you like," he said casually. "Limelight will enjoy following Rifka."

Our transition from trot to canter was a little jerky and I realized I was holding my pony's head too tight again, but when I relaxed and sat very still and light before folding forward from the hips, he took the jump perfectly. We had a fabulous time, hopping over fallen logs, ditches, and even some low-growing bushes.

"He cleared that one like a champion," Sean said admiringly. "Hey look, there's a stream up ahead; we'll take them in for a paddle."

"Can't we just jump it?" I was enjoying myself tremendously.

"We could but I'd like to see if Limelight trusts you enough to walk through this."

I could see the tension in my horse's neck muscles as I turned him toward the stream. It was broad and fairly shallow, gurgling pleasantly over its bed of pebbles. Sean moved Rifka forward, walking him into the middle then turning to walk along the length, the crystal-clear water swirling around the horse's knees. Limelight went in all right but stopped when he was only pastern-deep.

"Lots of encouragement, legs and voice, make yourself

sound very sure about it." Sean was watching from down-stream.

I made myself send out strong, positive vibes, letting my pony know that although I was aware we were doing something different, I had decided there was nothing to worry about and we were to move on. To my delight Lime-light responded to this "herd leader" demonstration and was soon wading knee-deep along the middle of the stream to join Rifka.

"That's terrific, and you can tell him so." Sean grinned at my delighted expression. "You two are coming along just great."

It was just a perfect afternoon for me, and when we arrived back at the paddock and watched Limelight and Rifka enjoy a vigorous roll before trotting off to join their friends, I thought nothing could spoil my day. Wrong again! Before we'd even got to the house Hannah came flying out to meet us, her face blotchy with tears.

"I'm phoning Dad to come and get us, Casey! I heard something horrible today and Molly just won't talk about it. I hate her and I want to go home!"

Chapter Seven

Although my first thought, selfishly, was, *No way, I love it here*, I'm glad to say my actual reaction was to fling my arms round her in total sympathy.

"Tell me what happened." I guided her toward the big hammock seat and sat her down.

Sean was shuffling his feet and looking embarrassed. I flapped a hand at him to go but Hannah said, "No, I want him to stay. You know Molly much better than I do, Sean, so maybe you can help."

"I can try," he said cautiously, sitting in a chair opposite us. "Go ahead."

"We—me and Mikey—went down to the beach outside Headley but it was real crowded, loads of people lying on the sand and kids in the water, so we went off to find somewhere quieter. We walked right round the bay and there was a nice little cove with just some fishing boats."

"Right," I said. My geography was a bit hazy, but I just about figured where she meant. "So you stayed there instead?"

"Yeah, we swam off some rocks and then went on the sand to dry. I was—" Her lower lip trembled, and she bit it to make it stop. "I was toweling my hair, it was all standing out like it does, and this—this horrible man doing something to a boat near us said, 'Molly? No, it can't be Molly,' and I said all cheerful, 'No I'm her niece Hannah.'"

"You do look just like her." I could feel she was still shaking. "So then what?"

"Then he—he kind of launched in at me and said our family had no right to come back to the cape where we'd done so much harm. He said people here didn't want us and we'd never get anyone to work in Forlorn House because they knew all the old ghosts would come back to haunt it now the Renshaws were living here again."

I blinked. "What old ghosts?"

"I don't *know.*" She was trying hard not to cry again. "Molly must know what he's talking about, she was fifteen when she left here so she has to remember. But she won't tell me. She just yelled that I shouldn't listen to prejudiced

81

idiots and slammed her door shut."

"She must be in shock," I said. "It's been a traumatic week for her, she's not thinking straight."

"My mum was right, I should never have come here." Poor Hannah was truly distressed. "If you'd seen this man at the cove, Casey—his face was all screwed up with hatred and it was directed at me!"

"He doesn't know you," Sean said—as ever, he was the voice of reason. "This is all tied up with family history and I think you're right—Molly has to tell you everything."

I totally agreed with him. "Come on, Hannah, we're all going to see your aunt and tell her she owes you an explanation."

"Okay." She gave one last sniff. "Mikey was great, told the fisherman to leave me alone and brought me back here, but when Molly started as well, I just ran off and left him."

"He'll understand," I said soothingly. "Let's go and get it sorted."

I wondered exactly how we were going to get an angry Molly to open her door but as soon as Sean tapped on it she opened up straight away.

"Hannah, I'm sorry." She held her niece close, swaying

unsteadily on her damaged leg. "I'm supposed to be the grown-up here and I bellowed at you like a spoiled kid. I didn't think I was ready to tell you, didn't think we knew each other well enough yet."

"If you two want to talk alone—" I said.

"No, I'm sure Hannah could do with a good friend like you for moral support." Molly limped back into the study. "And you come in too, Sean. I guess you're wondering exactly what kind of madhouse you're visiting, so I'd better tell all three of you."

As we entered the room my eyes were drawn instantly to the photo of Andrew Renshaw.

"Yes, you're right Casey." Molly hobbled to her chair. "My father is at the center of all this. Although his story's always haunted me, I stupidly thought twenty-five years was long enough for other folk to have forgotten. You know your grandfather died at sea, don't you, Hannah?"

She nodded. "In a boating accident—some kind of shipwreck, Mum said."

"And that's about all she did say, no doubt. She was only a little girl, you see; she just accepted what everyone told her and forgot about him. I think deliberately so. Unlike me she buried his memory, but—oh, anyway that's not the problem; I was just trying to explain why you don't know the whole story. It's the reason your mum and I fell out all those years ago. I wanted her to face the truth and she wouldn't."

"So what is the truth?"

Molly took a deep breath. "Your grandfather was skipper of a fishing boat, the *Lady Fair*. It was a family business—the Renshaws always lived on the cape and ran a fleet of boats. One night the *Lady Fair* went down in a storm off the northern cape. Two other men died and two survived, one being badly injured. The survivors told the inquest that the wreck was caused by Andrew Renshaw because he was drunk at the time and not capable of handling the boat. That's the story your mum didn't want you to know—the story that our father caused the death of two fine men and ruined the life of another."

There was a silence in the pretty room, a silence so deep I could hear my own heart beating.

"But that's—that's—horrible." Hannah's face was as white as a sheet. "No wonder that man on the beach hated me! And I didn't know, I didn't know!"

"I should have told you right away, darling. I'm so sorry." Molly was close to tears. "But it never occurred to me that you'd be attacked in that way. It's twenty-five years—I didn't dream local people would still remember, let alone despise us and take it out on you for looking like me. I just wanted to live back here. I've never felt at home anywhere else in the world, and I thought it would be all right. I told your mum so, that it was a new chapter in the family history, time to move on, all those things. I had no idea I was so, so wrong."

"Of course you didn't." I put an arm round both of them. "And it can *still* be a new beginning. This is a beautiful house in a beautiful place."

"Oh yeah, complete with its own haunting!" Hannah's eyes opened wide. "Is that why those women left—because they saw the ghosts of those men who drowned?"

"No!" Molly said angrily. "For a start, I don't believe in all that crap, and anyway Forlorn House ran successfully as a small hotel for years. Not one guest ever complained of being haunted."

"Maybe it's you—maybe it's *us*, not the house, that's stirring old ghost memories." Hannah was trembling again.

I was glad when Sean said firmly, "I'm with Molly on that one. Complete garbage! That fisherman probably spilled out his bit of vitriol about the Renshaw family and frightened two gullible local women into imagining ghostly happenings in the house."

"But there was the old man Sandy saw." Hannah was taking some convincing. "She said he didn't look normal."

"I still think that was the old boy who wanders round the grounds sometimes." Sean was being very reassuring.

"Yes, let's not get started on that." Molly looked uncomfortable. "The thing is, Hannah, what do you want to do? I really, really want you to stay, but I understand if you feel you have to leave."

I held my breath.

"I'll have to think." My friend turned away. "My head's all mixed up, I can't get anything straight."

"Let's go for a walk," I suggested. "Some fresh air might help clear it."

We left Sean with Molly and went back out into the garden. The sun was now low in the sky, burnishing the old stone of Forlorn House with a rosy glow. Hannah's pace was fast, and within minutes we reached the post and rails bordering the horses' paddock.

She climbed on the gate and turned to face the house. "You're right, Casey, it *is* a beautiful place."

From here you couldn't see the hotel extension, just the original old house with its high chimney and dipping gables.

"It kind of casts a spell," I agreed. "I think Molly wanted you to feel that."

"Yeah, right, but she could have warned me I'd be accused of being related to a murderer!"

"Even if the boat getting wrecked *was* your grandfather's fault, it doesn't make him that!" I was shocked.

"People died, didn't they, and what d'you mean *even if?*" She wasn't showing any sign of calming down.

"Well." I hesitated. "I know Molly told you the story straight out, including the bit about the survivors saying it was Andrew Renshaw's fault, but I get the feeling she doesn't really believe that. She loved her dad, you can tell, and she still wants his picture in her room. It wasn't her fault you got set on by that fisherman. Like she told us, she thought the story was ancient history—didn't think some local nutter would recognize you and start ranting on."

Hannah was silent for several minutes. "You make a lot of sense but I'm still not sure if I want to stay here. It's been a shock, you know, and—oh no, there's Mikey!"

"I thought you liked him." I watched as the smiling figure approached.

"I do, so I don't want him seeing me looking like—like a pink-eyed rat."

"That smile of his is definitely not for any kind of rat." I slid off the fence. "He likes you too, and I know he'll want you to stay."

"Don't move because of me, Casey." Mikey's friendly, engaging grin was a tonic. "I just wanted to make sure Hannah was okay. She was really upset earlier and I've been looking all over for her."

"Sorry, I guess I kinda lost it when Molly wouldn't tell me why that fisherman said all those things."

"I've always been told I have a sympathetic ear and a broad shoulder to cry on," Mikey said solemnly. "Personally I think that makes me sound like I'm deformed but you're welcome to use both if you like."

"Now, there's an offer you can't refuse!" I smiled at my friend. "You heard my take on the story; why not try Mikey for a second opinion?"

"You don't want to hear about old family stuff, do you?" She looked at him.

He hopped up on the fence to join her. "Try me."

I winked at Hannah and took off across the field to have an early-evening cuddle with Limelight. He was enjoying the fading warmth of the sun and leaned blissfully against me when I rubbed his ears and tickled his neck in the spot he liked best. I spent ages with him, not going back to the house till long shadows spread across the grass as the sun started dipping below the horizon. I could see Hannah and Mikey making their way back to the house too, heads close together as they talked. Even from here I could see the out-line of her mass of hair. I squinted hard to see if his arm was around her.

It was then I saw the man, well hidden from the house behind a clump of low-growing trees, his face turned to-ward the oblivious young couple only a few feet away. It was too far away to see his features or read the expression on his face but I could make out a full, graying beard and see that despite the weather he wore a hood pulled up over his head. For a horrible moment I thought he was going to pounce, that he was going to attack my friend or something, and I started to run, calling out her name. So deeply engrossed were they that neither Hannah nor Mikey heard, but to my relief they kept on walking and soon disappeared inside the house. I kept running until I reached the belt of trees, then hesitated, unsure whether to risk searching for the strange figure while I was all alone.

"You look hot," Sean called out. I turned to face him, panicky and incoherent. "When I say hot, I mean—" He was pretty incoherent himself. "—well, I mean overheated, though I do actually think you look hot and—"

"Sean, the old man, the one who scared Sandy and made Ozzie spook, he was here—hiding in those trees!"

"You stay here." He went straight into dynamic mode and ran toward the trees. I could hear him crashing around and was relieved when he came out shaking his head. "Nothing there. Are you sure you saw him?"

"Absolutely. I was way back in the field, but I was looking at Hannah and Mikey and spotted him."

"What was he doing?"

"Nothing." I shivered suddenly. "Just—watching."

"Oh Lord, Molly could definitely do without some old

weirdo around the place. Especially with the student we've got coming tomorrow."

"Another one?" I'd noticed a couple of empty rooms.

"Yeah. Molly said she told the girl no to start with, didn't want all the hassle, but the girl kept on and on, sent her a load of pictures of the work she's already done, and this morning Molly gave in and said okay. Now she's wishing she hadn't, of course, because she'd like to spend more time with Hannah if she gets the chance."

"I suppose with her injury she's confined to the house so she probably felt she had plenty of time," I said. "But what's the big deal with this particular student?"

"She's Summer Fenton." He said it as though he expected me to react, but I didn't. "*Fenton*," he emphasized. "Mean anything?"

I shook my head.

"She's the daughter of Matt Fenton—film star—that's got to ring some bells."

"Matt Fenton. Wow!" I was dead impressed. "My mum thinks he's yummy and—hey, wasn't there stuff in the paper about his daughter?"

"Yeah." Sean sounded grim. "There was a kidnap attempt on her last year when she was sixteen. It was foiled but her dad's been paranoid ever since—one of the reasons Molly wasn't keen on her coming. Summer now travels everywhere with a bodyguard, and we've got him too."

"That's why the weird old guy hanging around is definitely not good news!" I understood now. "On the other hand, a big burly bodyguard might be just the thing to scare old bogeyman away."

"That's one way of looking at it." His grin was back in place. "You can't say this place is dull, that's for sure."

I agreed and found myself hoping even more fervently that Hannah would decide to stay—life at Forlorn House was getting more exciting by the minute!

Chapter Eight

I didn't have to wait long to find out. Hannah had gone straight in to see her aunt, and together they came to join us in the big living room. My friend was still a bit pale but I could tell from the way she stood very close to Molly, almost physically supporting her, that she'd made up her mind to stay. Although four of us now knew about the tragedy surrounding Andrew Renshaw's death, there was no reason to share Molly's secret with the other students. When Toby and Paul came in, peeling off motorbike leathers, they found that the main topic of conversation was the imminent arrival of Summer Fenton.

"No way!" Toby punched the air with excitement. "I saw her picture in the paper—she is *gorgeous!*"

"Well, she can afford to be," Heather sniffed. "All those millions her devoted daddy spends on her."

"Media photographs are always airbrushed anyway,"

Sandy chimed in. "She's probably quite ordinary."

But Summer, when she arrived next morning, was far from that. She had her famous father's coloring, the brilliant blue eyes and tawny hair we'd seen on a thousand posters. She was tall like him too, but with a slender, feminine elegance that, combined with skin like rose petals and a smile so bright you could see your reflection in it, made her—well, just a complete knockout. The guys succumbed immediately, with Toby and Paul practically drooling while even the laid-back Sean and Mikey gulped and shuffled about excitedly. Summer didn't seem to notice. From across the studio, where she and the enormous, silent bodyguard arrived midway through the lesson, she spotted Molly and made straight for her.

"I expect everyone says it"—even her voice was attractively husky—"but I am your greatest fan, Miss Renshaw. My pop gave me your sculpture of *Summer* when I was fourteen and it totally changed my life."

"Summer?" Molly frowned slightly. "I don't remember—"

"He bought it at your London exhibition. It's the figure of a young woman, dancing."

"Of course." Molly extended her slightly mucky hand. "Um—you do know it symbolizes the season—I—er—didn't model it on you."

The girl's peal of laughter was natural and unself-conscious. "I should say! If I thought I was half that beautiful I'd be ecstatic! I was so excited by it I went out that day and bought some clay and a book called *How to Sculpt.*"

"Well done," Molly said heartily, trying not to look overwhelmed. "I'll be very interested to see what you produce in these sessions, especially with materials you've not tried before."

She went on to tell Summer everyone's name and then gave the little introductory speech we'd heard the day before.

"Cool. So I can start with a subject and a technique of my choice?" The girl took up a place on a bench between Toby and Paul, and I had to choke back a laugh at the expression of tortured bliss that crossed both their faces. "No contest then. I'll do a portrait head in clay."

"A portrait of whom?"

"Of my pop. He's such a doll and I love him to bits. It'll be a thank-you for letting me come here even though he's scared to death every time I'm out of the house."

"Ah yes." Molly seemed to have forgotten the enormous silent companion. "You haven't introduced us to Mr.—um—"

"He's Ivo. This is my bodyguard, everyone, he doesn't say much but he worries a lot. He's a very nice guy and he'll try not to make anyone feel uncomfortable."

"Pleased to meet you, Ivo." Molly politely held out the charcoal-stained hand again. "So you'll be with Summer all the time?"

"Yes ma'am, wherever she goes, I go." His voice was surprisingly soft.

"Good," Molly said vaguely, obviously slightly lost in a situation she hadn't come across before. "You'll be joining our classes then?"

"Yes ma'am, but not participating."

"Right, everyone, we'll all carry on, shall we? Summer and—um—Ivo, would you like to freshen up first or—"

"No I want to get stuck right in." Summer took off her pink designer jacket and climbed into one of Molly's white overalls.

Toby and Paul watched her with rapt concentration and I heard a great sigh of irritation from Sandy. I carried on making the base for my tree with Molly showing me how to bend the aluminum wire I needed. The rest of the morning went by in a flash and to my surprise it was soon lunchtime. Toby and Paul, having run all over the studio fetching and carrying for Summer, now jostled to get next to her at the table and were noticeably put out when she chose to sit between Molly and the ever-present Ivo.

"Molly, seeing I've already missed a class and a half could I please have a short session this afternoon?" she sweetly pleaded.

"I don't think so, I've already promised Hannah I'd go to the school and lend a hand with Mikey's riding lesson."

"*Riding?* You teach horseback riding too?"

"Not officially. I'd normally be taking one of my own ponies off across the cape, but my stupid accident put a stop to that. My niece is showing Mikey here how to ride. She and Casey have brought their own horses along for the duration."

"So have we, my brother and me," Toby put in eagerly. "If you want to ride out I'll be glad to accompany you, Summer."

"Me on a horse? No thanks!" Again the peal of laughter. "I'm a complete klutz with any sports, and horses are a definite no."

"So what's your favorite hobby?" Toby wasn't giving up. "How about a spin on a Harley? Now, that's real excitement."

"I'll take your word for it but I don't think Ivo would be too keen. I'm happy just to laze around when I'm not sculpting."

"I have some great books on sandstone and a rare one on the use of *ciment fondu*," Paul said quickly. "I could show you those if you like."

"Sure." She smiled good-humoredly. "What are the rest of you up to? Will you all be galloping about on your horses?"

"Sandy and I will probably go to the beach," Heather said. "It's good swimming, but I guess you're not allowed, are you?"

"Oh, maybe if there aren't too many people around. Ivo doesn't like crowds—they make his job too difficult."

"Is there a quieter place away from the tourist spots?" Paul asked, still patently besotted.

"There are several," Molly put in quickly. "Not to the

south, one's always full of families and the other's for local fishermen. Hannah and her friends can show you a quiet bay if you don't mind climbing down a cliff."

"Duh!" Summer held up her hands in horror. "I'm a lazy girl, me, I don't do climbing, and I can swim every day in our pool at home if I want, so I'm truly not bothered. Nice of you all to offer, though, and—hey, this lunch is great, isn't it? Good food and the fantastic Molly Renshaw—what else could I possibly need?"

I thought she was terrific, genuinely sweet and funny, but after she left us to "go and take a lie-down" it was clear not everyone felt the same.

"Well!" Sandy sounded highly indignant. "What a spoiled little madam *she* is! Demanding an extra lesson from poor injured Molly."

"She didn't exactly demand," Molly pointed out. "And she didn't seem to mind when I said I was helping Hannah instead."

"She'll probably offer you money." Heather was sour-faced too. "That type thinks the almighty dollar is the answer to everything."

"If I do it, it'll be because I want to," Molly said crisply.

"Summer is extremely talented, that's why she's here, not because she has a rich father."

"Yeah, right," Heather muttered.

Toby made an impatient movement. "Give the girl a break."

"I might have known you'd be on Little Miss Movie Star's side, Toby," Sandy snapped. "It was embarrassing the way you were at her beck and call all lesson. She's perfectly capable of doing her own fetching and carrying—she *does* have legs, you know!"

"Oh boy, she sure has!" Toby said reverently, which made Sean crack up laughing.

"Behave yourself, you lot." Molly tried to sound stern. "You sound like a bunch of kids from nursery school instead of the group of mature, sensitive students I thought I'd enrolled."

"We're okay," Hannah said, looking at her aunt. "Don't worry, no one has it in for Summer really, she's just a bit much to take in first off. I think she's great but I'm glad she doesn't ride. If she was perfect at that too it just wouldn't be fair!"

We laughed, except Heather and Sandy who were still

looking thoroughly disgruntled. They set off for the beach once again after looking unsuccessfully for Toby and Paul in the hope the two guys would join them.

"My brother's on the computer upstairs, researching everything he can find about sculpture so he can impress Summer," Sean said with a chuckle. "And I bet Paul's sitting outside her room with his rare book in the hope she'll let him read it to her."

"Sad, aren't they?" Mikey joined in his laughter. "All that effort just to get a girl's attention—hey, what am I saying?—I'm spending the next hour bouncing around on a horse so I can interest my girl!"

I raised my eyebrows at this nineteen-year-old's use of *my girl* and wondered wistfully if Sean's interest in sorting Limelight's problems was because he liked my horse—or me. His help was certainly invaluable; Molly, after watching him work on our leg yielding, was impressed.

"You're in safe hands there, Casey," she told me. "Sean's improving not just your technique but also the relationship you have with your pony. A better rider makes a better horse, and a horse that trusts his rider is far less likely to get into trouble the way Limelight used to."

She left us practicing and limped heavily over to the other side of the school where Hannah was putting Mikey through some warm-up exercises. We moved on to shoulder-in at trot, which Sean said was a great help with a fizzy, forward-going type like Limelight.

"It teaches your horse to accept your leg aid without running away from it, as it's obviously not so easy to run sideways!" He grinned at us both encouragingly.

I liked the way he not only taught me stuff, but explained why and how it would benefit Limelight and me. I enjoyed the work and afterward was much more relaxed when Sean suggested another ride out.

"Across the cape or down the beach—your choice." He saddled Rifka up very quickly.

"Cape, I think. I really enjoyed the country stuff yesterday, especially the jumping."

In exploring mode, we set off along a different track and were soon cantering through a beautiful wooded valley. To our delight someone had already set up some small logs, positioning them between a long line of trees so they formed a fantastic jumping lane. We started off with me following Sean, taking the staggered set of jumps a few paces behind him so Limelight wouldn't get over-excited and try to belt past. My pony really enjoyed it, and we were both so relaxed and confident that we took the lead the next time. Apart from getting a little strong and pulling excitedly at the end of the lane, Limelight did really well and I praised him extravagantly, even lying along his neck and kissing his ears.

"You're daft about that horse," Sean said teasingly. "There'd be guys queuing up for that sort of treatment, you know!"

I blushed and felt something lovely whiz and thunder around in my insides like a firework going off. I was feeling pretty darn great when we left the little valley and found ourselves riding along the top of some awesomely steep, jagged cliffs. Below us the ocean pounded against a rocky outcrop, throwing white torrents of spray skyward as the waves broke against the slabs of slate gray.

"The tide's coming in," Sean pointed out. "Soon those rocks will be completely covered. You can see why this is such a dangerous piece of coast."

"Is this where the *Lady Fair* got wrecked, d'you suppose?" I looked down and shuddered. "A boat foundering on those rocks wouldn't stand a chance."

"I guess it must have been somewhere around here," Sean agreed. "Come on. I think we'd better start making our way back."

We turned the horses and trotted them a few yards in from the cliff edge, following a rough track that wound through a series of small rocks and boulders. Taking the next curve at a brisk working trot, I spotted the familiar, hooded figure before Limelight did. The old man was away to our left on the cliff edge, looking down at the sea below. He seemed to be holding something and he suddenly dropped it, sending it spinning and ricocheting loudly against the cliff face. In the split second before my horse saw him, I tensed instantly, tightening my hands and stiffening my back and legs. Limelight reacted, turning his head, neck muscles twitching, as he veered violently to the right, away from the weird, ghostly shape on the cliff. I tried to stay with him but tension made my seat precarious, and I felt myself slipping, hands clutching wildly at the air as I fell. My one thought was to grab for Limelight's trailing reins—but as the rocky ground came up to hit me I knew it was just too late.

Chapter Nine

Limelight was out of sight before, completely winded, I managed to raise my head. Sean was at my side in an instant.

"Don't move," he commanded. "Just lie still so I can check nothing's broken."

Taking great gulps of air, I tried to gasp that I was fine, but he carried on running gentle yet firm hands over my legs and arms.

"That's very nice," I finally managed to croak. "But I'd rather you went and caught Limelight."

"And leave you?" His worried face softened as he smiled at me. "No chance. Anyway chasing your horse will only make him run faster. He'll head straight for home, don't worry."

Thinking of the sheer cliffs bordering the trip "home" I couldn't help but worry, but there was nothing I could do about it. I sat up, still gasping as I tried to refill my lungs. "Where's that old man now? I want to give him a mouthful for scaring my horse like that."

Sean looked around. "He's gone. And to be honest—" He hesitated. "He didn't actually *do* anything. He had his back to us, looking down at the sea, so he didn't spook Limelight deliberately."

"Oh, that's all right then." I scrambled bad-temperedly to my feet. "As long as he didn't mean it."

"Is your knee okay?" Sean frowned as I took a few steps. "You're limping a bit."

"It's just stiff—it's the one I hurt last time I came off." I rubbed it gingerly. "I can walk, though."

"Don't be nuts. You ride Rifka and I'll walk."

"Why? It's not your fault I have a crazy pony who shies at anything that moves." I was really, *really* cranky.

"No one's to blame; it's just one of those things. Don't get discouraged, we're going to make a model horse out of Limelight, remember?"

"Yeah, sure." I moved a few more steps, and he put a hand out to stop me.

"Look, if you don't want me to walk how about I give

you a lift home? You can sit behind me, which means you'll have to put your arms round me, I guess. But if you can bear to do that . . ." He gave me his wonderful grin and despite the mood I was in I felt that lovely trembly sensation again.

I managed a smile and soon we were both astride Rifka's strong back as he picked his way along the rocky track.

"You're sure Limelight will know which way to go?" My face was very close to the back of Sean's head; when he turned slightly I was nearly touching his cheek with my mouth.

"Horses have a built-in instinct for even a temporary home," he said, very reassuring. "Limelight will take the shortest, most direct route and be at Forlorn House way before we are."

Our progress was slow with Rifka staying at a steady walk while I, sitting very close, snuggled against Sean's warm body. I kept on worrying about Limelight, of course; I just couldn't help it. I tried not to imagine him galloping over a cliff, or hurtling into a tree, or maybe even getting himself hopelessly lost. Sean was right again, though, for when we rode out of the wooded part of Molly's grounds and started approaching the paddock we could see a group of people clustered round the unmistakable silver figure of my pony.

"Casey!" Hannah ran toward us, a huge smile of relief lighting her face. "You're okay! I was just about to get Toby so we could ride out and find you."

"I told you she'd be fine with Sean." Molly was holding Limelight's lead rope.

He turned his handsome head to me and whinnied loudly.

"He's telling you he's pleased to see you." Summer was there, though standing well back. "Ivo spotted him running and we came over and got him then called Molly to check him over."

"Thanks very much, Summer." I tried to hide my surprise.

"Oh, I didn't do anything." She smiled disarmingly. "Ivo got hold of his bridle, then Hannah took all his gear off and they've been checking him out ever since."

"He's got a couple of minor scratches is all," Molly said briskly. "What about you, Casey?"

"I'm fine, just injured pride that I couldn't stay on when

he spooked."

"He didn't just run then?" Hannah watched me slide a bit stiffly off Rifka's back. "Something scared him, did it?"

"Yeah, and it was that old man's fault again," I said vengefully. "The same one who caused Molly's accident."

"Uh, that's not quite true." Sean was painfully honest. "He didn't leap out this time—he was just *there*."

"Where? What old man?" Ivo was suddenly vigilant. "Is there a problem I don't know about, Molly?"

"No problem." She glared at me. "There's a harmless old guy who wanders around on the cape. Casey's just being over-dramatic."

I opened my mouth to argue but realized I'd be causing trouble and shut it again.

"We were way north on the cape when it happened," Sean assured Ivo. "Nowhere near the house, so you don't have to worry about Summer."

"That's okay then." Summer stretched like a contented cat. "I can go back to my sunbathing now, Ivo. Glad you and your horse are okay, Casey."

We watched her saunter back to the hammock in the garden, followed by the enormous Ivo who, even in shorts and T-shirt, couldn't be anything but a bodyguard.

Molly handed me Limelight's rope and said tersely, "Here you are. Can you just be a bit more careful in future?" and limped heavily away.

"Ooh, 'scuse my grumpy old aunt." Hannah opened the field gate for me. "It's not like you came off Limelight deliberately."

"I think she meant I should watch what I say, especially in front of Ivo." I led my horse into the paddock. "He's forever on the lookout for trouble, guess he thinks even a strange old man is a potential threat." I felt guilty now for shouting my mouth off. "So Molly's right, I shouldn't have said anything."

"There's no harm done," Hannah said peacefully. "Ivo's not going to be worried about an old guy on the cape. Summer's not exactly the type to go hiking out there, is she?"

We laughed and I gave my wayward pony one last pat before releasing him. He seemed totally unconcerned about his solo flight back to the house and took off across the grass with Rifka as if he hadn't a care in the world.

"Don't worry." Sean was watching my face. "We'll do

some more work in the school tomorrow, try and find out just what it is that gets him scared."

"Thanks, Sean." I tried not to be downhearted.

We'd arranged a trip into Headley for a meal out in the evening. I felt a lot better once I'd showered off all the day's dust and grime and got dressed up.

"Wow!" Hannah was fixing her hair. "You look gorgeous. I hope Sean appreciates what a lucky guy he is."

"I'm not trying to impress Sean," I lied. "Anyway what about you? You look like a glam rocker with all that sparkly stuff in your hair."

"Thanks, pal." She pulled a hideous face. "I was actually going for sophisticated, not freaky."

"Oh sure," I said carelessly. "I guess you want to look older, don't you?"

"Older? Why?"

"Um, well, with Mikey being nineteen—I thought—"

"Well, don't think." She sounded quite sharp. "It doesn't suit you."

I shrugged and thought resentfully that Hannah seemed very touchy about Mikey's age. You had to watch every word you said in this place—there was always someone who seemed to take offense. Sandy and Heather were another case in point. Sandy had really dolled up—the works, heavy on the eyeliner—while Heather, scrubbed of face and dressed in old jeans, seemed to be making a different kind of statement.

"I don't know why you've all bothered," she said, glaring at us. "Summer Fenton will come floating along dressed in a five-thousand-dollar frock with real diamonds in her ears and make you all look like trailer trash."

"Garbage!" Sean said hotly. "Case—I mean they all look great."

"Fabulous." Mikey's eyes were fixed on Hannah, and I saw her smile at him.

Summer did, of course, look wonderful, and the besotted Toby and Paul were practically doing circus tricks vying for her approval, while Heather and Sandy managed to look disparaging and jealous at the same time. Despite all these complications I had a lovely evening talking and laughing with Sean in the quaint little seafood restaurant we visited. It was on the outskirts of Headley, an area less crowded and touristy than the center and harbor front, Molly told us.

"The town's grown enormously while I've been away," she said. "I haven't been down here much, what with working on the house, then breaking my ankle, but I've noticed the changes."

"Twenty-five years is a long time." Hannah seemed to be getting on very well with her aunt, I was pleased to see. "I expect there are a lot more tourists for a start."

"Yep, haven't seen one familiar face." Molly was limping toward our waiting taxi. "Even the cabdriver's from Manchester, he was telling me, and—"

"Molly Renshaw!" It was more a snarl than a greeting. "And all your little hangers-on."

"Excuse me?" Molly stopped short and stared at the gray-haired, black-browed man blocking the sidewalk. "Do I know you?"

"You should, but then you Renshaws always did think you were better than the rest of us. And now you're some kind of famous artist you think it's all right to come back here, do you?" He leaned forward, looking menacing, but the enormous bulk of Ivo suddenly blocked his way.

"Is there a problem?" The bodyguard was shielding Summer from the man's sight.

"Not for me, buddy." The older man backed off immediately. "If you're staying at Forlorn House it's you who's got the problem."

Ivo watched him disappear down a side alley and, without turning his head, said, "In the car, Summer. I'll talk to you back at the house, Molly."

Still carefully shielding the girl he guided her back to the big car, followed by a bemused-looking Toby and Paul, who'd hitched a ride. The rest of us scrambled into two waiting taxis with Molly, Hannah, and Mikey in one, while Sean and I shared the other with Sandy and Heather.

"Well!" Sandy said. "What was all that about? That man really had it in for Molly by the sound of it."

"Didn't you love the way Ivo swung into action?" Heather, for some reason, seemed to find it funny. "Straight out of the movies with his one phrase—*Is there a problem?* The guy was scared witless."

"Just as well," Sandy sniffed. "Otherwise there would have been real trouble. Did you *see* the way he was looking at Molly? If looks could kill . . ."

I shuddered at the expression and Sean squeezed my hand comfortingly. We didn't join in the girls' speculation, but as soon as got back to the house I rushed to find Hannah.

"Is Molly okay?"

"Bit shaken." My friend looked a little pale herself. "You probably gathered that was the same guy who went for me on the beach."

"Yes, I guessed. So who is he?"

Hannah shrugged. "Molly says his face is familiar but she can't recall his name. He's obviously a local who was here when the *Lady Fair* sank and he still blames my grandfather for it."

"Phew, long memories—it's like a vendetta you read about in books," I said, giving her a hug. "Don't let it get to you. It's all in the past—that man will just have to learn to leave it there and move on the way Molly has."

"Mm, I think Molly's having more trouble doing that than she thought," Hannah said. "She's in the study with Ivo now, trying to convince him everything's okay."

"I can't see the story being a threat to Summer, which is Ivo's only concern." I was trying hard to cheer her up. "I mean, tonight must have worried him with that guy suddenly appearing and laying into Molly, but it's not as if Summer was the target."

"Ivo doesn't want any kind of trouble, period." My friend ran her fingers through her curls, forgetting the expensive gel. "Duh, now look what I've done! And Mikey really liked my hair done this way."

I laughed at the face she was making. "It's worth doing again then, isn't it? Come on, I'll give you a hand so you're all beautiful again."

We ran upstairs to her room, where she quickly grabbed the tube of gel. She was peering intently in the mirror as I moved over to close the curtains so she didn't see the start I made. Outside the sky was a black velvet cloak bejeweled with stars, while the silver disk of the moon shed light across the garden below me. There, her wild mane of hair clearly outlined, was Molly, leaning on her stick as she bent forward to talk to someone. I saw her check furtively behind her, glancing anxiously at the house before she limped forward and was swallowed up by the darkness. It was the someone she was joining that made me jump. Even with his bearded face half hidden in the shadows I could see it was the unmistakable figure of the hooded man—the man she'd assured us would never be seen around Forlorn House again!

Chapter Ten

"Come on, Casey," Hannah said impatiently. "What are you doing?"

"Nothing." I drew the curtains sharply. "I'll give you a hand."

I stood behind her, scrunching the back of her hair and thinking about what I'd just seen. My first instinct had been to call my friend to the window, but I'd stopped myself when I saw the secretive way Molly had gone to join the old man. Her attitude toward him was hard to understand, but it was clear his presence around the place was something she didn't want made public. I liked Molly a lot but found her pretty scary sometimes and didn't want to risk annoying her by blabbing again. Much better, I thought, to have a quiet word; then maybe she'd explain just who the old man was.

"*Casey!*" Hannah roared.

I stopped scrunching and said, "Huh?"

"That's three times I asked you to stop—my hair's fine. You were miles away. Thinking about Sean, were you?"

"No."

"Yes you were, ooh isn't love wonderful!" Clowning around, she pretended to pump her heart.

"Well you'd know," I retorted, throwing a pillow at her. "Getting your hair glammed up twice in one night! You must have it real bad for Mikey."

Shoving and pushing each other jokily we ran back downstairs to meet up with the others. I was pleased to see that Sean and Mikey were on one side of the big living room while the rest of the students were in a huddle at the other end.

"What're you doing?" Hannah tossed her sparkly head and sat down next to them.

"Sean's going to teach me a new card game." Mikey shuffled up so he was very close to her. "Want to join in?"

"What are Summer and the others up to?" I looked at Sean.

"She's got this fabulous book of sculpture exhibits; it must have cost a fortune. Heather and Sandy are dead irritated she's got it but can't bear not to look."

"While Toby and Paul are just spending the time looking at Summer," I laughed, feeling ridiculously glad Sean didn't seem to have caught the Summer obsession. Although I was happy to join in the card game I kept a lookout for Molly's reappearance. She'd been so positive the old man was harmless, I couldn't believe she was in any real danger, but when at last I saw her limping toward us I heaved a sigh of relief.

"Are you all okay?" Molly's smile was a bit tired, I thought.

"Yep. You?" Hannah put an affectionate arm around her aunt. "I was worried that horrible fisherman had upset you so much you'd gone to bed."

"No, I'm determined not to let him get to me. I—just went for a wander round the studio."

I don't think she noticed the start I gave, but Sean did. I saw him frown.

"So what do you think of my bird sculpture?" Hannah asked. "Is it any good?"

"Can't tell yet but this piece is all about expressing yourself anyway. If it pleases you it's fine, doesn't matter what

I think."

"That's cool—no criticism. What about the next project?" Mikey wanted to know.

"That'll be tougher, but I'll be helping with the technical side of things and—yes, Heather, did you want me?"

Heather, it appeared, had gotten into an argument with Paul over one of the illustrations in Summer's book and wanted Molly's opinion. By the time she'd sorted that out it was pretty late and I found myself getting ready for bed without having had the quiet chat I'd intended.

Molly was obviously keeping tonight's visit from Weirdo Man a secret, I told myself. I still thought I'd better wait and talk to her before I told anyone what I saw.

The next morning gave me no chance either. After a noisy breakfast, with Heather and Paul carrying on the disagreement from the night before, we went straight to the studio to work on our pieces. My armature was progressing very slowly. I'd finally managed a reasonable drawing of the tree I wanted to sculpt but found the twisting technique Molly showed me, where I transferred the shape into binding wire, very hard to achieve. Heather had finished her much larger and more complicated armature of a horse, had padded out the torso and legs with strips of wood, and was now wrapping binding wire loosely around the whole thing, apparently to help the clay to grip. Before I'd started this class I thought you just got a lump of clay and wiggled it around into roughly the right shape, but I was quickly learning there was a whole lot more to it. Even Sean's carving—easy enough, you'd think, just take your lump of wood and start sawing or chiseling—but no. He'd made a template of his horse from stiff card, which, now that he was satisfied with it, would be transferred to the block for carving.

Everyone in the room was busy, including, for the first time, Ivo. Previously the bodyguard had simply sat near Summer's bench, glancing occasionally at a magazine, while he kept a tight vigil. Today he'd brought in a laptop computer and was working on it right next to her. This meant Toby was now separated from his beloved so he kept glancing irritably at Ivo, which meant he often dropped the strange assortment of objects he was fusing together to make his abstract. I met up with him when I went to fetch more wire.

"That Ivo's a moron," he said glumly as he picked up a tube of silicone sealer. "I think I'll ask Molly to make him move. He's—er—blocking out my light."

"And spoiling your view of Summer," I said in mock sympathy.

"Yeah, well, and that. It means Paul's got her practically to himself this morning. I bet he asks her out."

"Oh well, console yourself with the thought that if she says yes it means Ivo gets to go on the date too." I grinned at him. "Not exactly romantic!"

Toby gave a half smile. "Guess not. I'd settle for it, though."

He really did have it bad, I thought as I made my way back to my embryo sculpture. I noticed that Summer had several photos, head shots of her film-star father, pinned on a board in front of her to help her sculpt a good likeness, so I stepped forward to take a look. Matt Fenton's a bit old, of course, but still a very good-looking man, and I wondered if his daughter's clay portrait was going to do him justice. As I moved away I glanced at the screen on Ivo's computer and stopped abruptly. Another face glowered out at me, no handsome movie star this time, but the gray hair and black brows above grizzled, downturned features were still familiar. It was the man we'd seen outside the restaurant in Headley—the fisherman who'd ranted first at Hannah then at Molly that the Renshaw family weren't welcome back on the Cape. I couldn't wait till lunchtime to tell Hannah.

"Ivo's in the study with Molly right now," she said. "I'll go and find out what it's all about."

We had to wait till we'd eaten and were heading off to the horses' field before she got a chance to tell us.

"Ivo's been doing some detective work. He didn't like the way that bloke looked at us last night so he'd been finding out about him."

"So who is he?" Mikey was carrying Rafferty's saddle and bridle.

"His name's Skeet Sanders—Molly said she knew the name as soon as Ivo said it. And get this—*Skeet was aboard the* Lady Fair *the night she sank off the cape!*"

"No! How come Molly didn't recognize him?" I asked. "I'd have thought even at fifteen she'd know her father's crew members."

"He wasn't a regular, stepped in to help out that night apparently and no wonder he's so anti-Renshaw, he's one of only two survivors from the wreck. He's got firsthand knowledge that the accident was my grandfather's fault." Hannah was speaking very quietly. "So you can understand him hating us."

"What's Ivo going to do about it now he knows this Skeet's background?" Sean asked. "He's not taking Summer away, is he?"

"No. Molly said she didn't like Ivo knowing about that part of our family history but Ivo was totally nonjudgmental. Said it was all in the past, with no bearing on Summer, and if it became 'a problem' he'd simply tell Skeet Sanders to stay away."

"And from what we saw last night old Skeet will do just that," Mikey said. "He's brave enough when it comes to shouting at women, but he got out of the way pretty quick when Ivo got involved."

"Yeah, well, you would, wouldn't you?" Sean laughed. "He's got some great organization behind him, our bodyguard chum, hasn't he? Being able to call up Skeet Sanders's record like that."

"I expect he's checked us all out." I climbed onto the gate and whistled for Limelight. "He'd have made sure he wasn't bringing Summer to a place teeming with criminals, wouldn't he?"

There was a crash followed by a string of swear words as Mikey, still holding the tack, fell noisily off the gate. Hannah rushed to help him while Sean and I somewhat unkindly jeered a bit as we walked away to get our horses. Limelight, wouldn't you know it, was a complete angel in the school, going through his routine of warm-up lateral work and twenty-meter circles.

"Seeing he's in such a good mood, how about we try him with a swim again?"

Although pleased with his performance, I wasn't too sure.

"Go on, Casey," Hannah urged. "It's fantastic—you'll love it."

"Don't you miss out either, Han." Mikey seemed none the worse for his tumble, though I noticed he and Hannah had gone into one of their huddles and shared a long, secretive discussion about something when she helped him to his feet.

"You could ride Khan and lead Rafferty, Hannah," Sean said. "My love-struck brother is staying in the garden so he can make up ground with Summer."

"Would he mind me riding his horse?" Han was well up for it.

"You'd be doing him a favor. The dopey sap isn't giving Khan enough exercise, is he? I'll double-check if you're worried and get the saddle if you want."

He quickly returned with Khan's tack, and soon all four of us were riding very sedately through the grounds of Forlorn House.

"Don't worry about me," Mikey, looking confident but very novicey, called. "Do what you usually do and I'll keep up."

He didn't want to be led, though I saw Hannah put a rope in her pocket just in case. She looked quite tiny, perched high on Khan's lofty chestnut back, but was thoroughly enjoying the novelty. It was another glorious day, the afternoon sun beating down in hot waves as the four horses picked their way carefully along the narrow track. Rafferty plodded dutifully behind Khan, not seeming to mind carrying a complete beginner, and Limelight, still in perfectly obedient mode, behaved beautifully as lead horse. Sean brought up the rear so he could watch out for any trouble, but until we were actually approaching the cliff edge everything was just fine.

I'd increased the pace to negotiate one of the verdant grassy patches, just a medium trot, but Mikey, bouncing about, managed to lose his reins. Rafferty, feeling the contact disappear, showed his usual inclination—not to bolt, buck, or swerve but to put his head straight down and eat. Poor Mikey, completely unbalanced, fell forward in a slow, graceless slide down the bay pony's neck to end in a crumpled heap right next to Rafferty's still-munching jaws. He looked so funny the rest of us burst out laughing. Hannah hopped off Khan to wave the lead rope at him.

"Told you we might need this, Mikey!"

"Aw, Han I'd feel like a dopey kid with that on." He brushed himself down and clambered back aboard. "I'll try harder, honest."

I thought he'd have a fit when he saw the steep cliff path but if he was scared he didn't show it, and he and Rafferty managed the descent really well. Sean, stripping off his T-shirt, looked as though he couldn't wait to get in the ocean, but insisted on staying with me.

"Ride close beside us and give him loads of encouragement. I just know Limelight's going to swim today."

But sadly Limelight had other ideas. Again he showed no desire to run and didn't shy or spook at anything. He did nothing at all, in fact. Despite all our efforts my wayward, difficult pony refused point-blank to move more than fetlock-deep in the wonderful, welcoming ocean. Once again I had to watch from the shore as the others, including complete novice Mikey, splashed and cavorted and *swam* to their hearts' content!

Chapter Eleven

To say I was mad doesn't really describe it. After ten minutes or so Sean came back to the beach, took one look at my face, and said sympathetically, "You take Rifka and enjoy a good swim while I try to get your boy in."

I'm obviously every bit as stubborn as my horse because I heard myself say, "No thanks. *I* want to be the one to get Limelight in that ocean, and I want my first swim to be with him."

Sean blinked a bit but said he admired my determination.

"Yeah well"—I was totally fed up.—"it's obviously not enough, is it? You go back in, Sean, there's no need for you to miss out on the fun."

I turned Limelight and started riding along the beach away from him, trying to stop the tears of frustration. I heard Sean calling my name but I didn't want him feeling sorry for me and I genuinely had no intention of stopping him enjoying his swim, so I kept on going. Eventually he took Rifka out into the sea again. They stayed in longer this time, and I watched enviously from the shore as the three horses plunged strongly through the aquamarine water. Mikey, considering he didn't have the skill, balance, or experience of the other two, did amazingly well. He slid off Rafferty's back several times but managed to swim alongside the pony and scramble back on. Once Rafferty, swimming strongly out toward the open sea, left him behind, but Sean and Hannah, whooping and laughing, chased after the bay pony on Rifka and Khan and led him back. I thought it looked as though they were having the best time ever but told myself firmly I wasn't to sulk or be moody with them when they finally returned to join us. On the ride back to Forlorn House, Rifka, Khan, and Rafferty were pretty quiet, tired as they were from their swimming exertions. Limelight, of course, was still full of fizz and bounced eagerly, wanting to canter and gallop on.

"I'll take him round the little jumping course you set up," I told Sean. "He loves that, and it'll burn up some of this surplus energy."

"Okay." His dark, warm eyes looked into mine. "I'll

come over and help once I've washed all the salt off Rifka."

"Don't worry, I'll be fine—oh, there's Molly—maybe she'll give me a hand."

Molly seemed glad to have something to do. The enforced inactivity caused by her broken ankle really didn't suit her.

"Sorry if I'm cranky," she surprised me by saying as she limped along beside Limelight. "I'm sure I'd be coping a lot better with all the irritations that keep cropping up if I could get out and *do* more. I've so been looking forward to summer on the cape, the riding, the swimming—"

"Yeah well, talking of irritations—" I told her about my pony's refusal to go into the water.

"He's like Ozzie, a highly strung boy who thinks too much. Don't worry; you'll get him in there eventually."

"That's what Sean says, but it's so frustrating when I try to do everything right and Limelight still plays me up. Yet Rafferty was happy to go swimming with a complete beginner on his back."

"Different kind of horse altogether," Molly said briskly. "Frankly I'd rather have an Ozzie or a Limelight any day, even though I'm the first to admit they're not easy."

"That's true." I leaned forward and patted Limelight's neck. "Can we show you how our jumping's going? I think we've improved a lot."

Molly stood in the center of the school, leaning on her stick as she scrutinized every approach, takeoff, and landing. Her advice was spot-on; she seemed to know exactly what Limelight was thinking and put us right when we had trouble getting the bounce between two fences set up without a stride between them. We left the fenced-in school area and were walking across the field leading back to the yard, with Limelight on a long rein so he could stretch his neck muscles after all his hard work. Deeply engrossed in talking riding technique and looking down at Molly, I was completely unprepared when just ahead there came the sharp crack of a broken twig as a figure suddenly appeared from behind a tree. Limelight was half asleep, and it scared him so that he spooked and shied sideways. Flung violently out of the saddle I somehow managed to stay aboard, shorten my reins, and regain my seat.

"Oh, well *done*, Casey." Molly, moving as fast as she could, limped forward.

I knew it was the old man again, even before I'd

glimpsed the now familiar hooded top he wore. This time I was close enough to see his face, and to my absolute amazement I could clearly make out the tears that were trickling slowly from his cloudy eyes. Molly put her head close to his and spoke briefly and so quietly I couldn't make out the words. The old man raised a hand and stretched it toward me in a gesture that seemed to be an apology. Then he turned and disappeared back into the trees.

"Who—who the heck *is* that?" I slid off Limelight's back and led him over to join her. "I saw you meeting him last night, Molly, I was going to ask you then but—"

"I'd be very grateful if you didn't mention him," she said quickly. "I don't want the other students getting into a panic."

"But he's always turning up here, they're bound to see him," I objected.

She hesitated. "I suppose you're right, though I'm sure I've convinced him not to come near the house anymore, and I'll try to keep him out of the grounds too. I think last night he just wanted to make sure you were all right after your fall."

"But he caused—" I stopped. "No, that's not fair, he didn't do anything—he's just kind of scary the way he suddenly appears. Limelight was really good just now. Even though he spooked he didn't try and run off."

"That's right," Molly agreed. "And I think the old man was just checking you were okay."

"I still reckon you're going to have to tell the other guys about him. He's going to scare one of them, and then Ivo will worry he's a threat to Summer."

"Oh Lord," she groaned. "Why did I go and let all these complications into my life? You're right, of course; I'll have a quick word with everyone."

"And you'll tell us who he is?" I called but she was gone, limping rapidly toward the house, leaving me to lead Limelight back to his paddock.

I was feeling a lot more cheerful, pleased my pony hadn't gone into another terrifying bolt after his scare and optimistic I could sort out the swimming problem. As I released Limelight into the field Sean came over and tickled me under the chin.

"Hah, that's better! You look more like yourself now."

"Who did I look like before?" I inquired. "A miserable old crow I bet."

"You're not old," he said seriously.

I thumped him cheerfully with my riding helmet. "Thanks a lot! The jumping session went well, Molly was a big help. She says Limelight and I are doing fine so eventually I'll convince him to go in that ocean."

"Sure you will." He grinned encouragingly. "You two are really starting to bond. Oh look, there's my brother and Paul."

He pointed to where the Harley had just stopped outside the house.

"Where've you been?" Sean greeted them. "Don't tell me you followed Ivo."

The bodyguard, we knew, had taken Summer out for a drive.

"Fun–*nee*." Now it was Toby's turn to clout Sean. "Such a joker, aren't you? Paul and I went for a spin round the Cape."

"And I bought Summer some flowers." Paul reached inside his jacket and proudly brought out a bedraggled bouquet. "Oh no, they've got all battered!"

I saw Toby give a wicked grin. "Tough luck, buddy. You're not going to impress her with those, now, are you?"

"Impress who? Oh don't tell me—you've brought flowers for Summer!" A tanned Sandy had just returned from the beach. "You sad sap."

"Actually they're for you." Toby snatched up the bouquet and handed it to her with a flourish.

"What about me?" Heather demanded. "Or don't I count?"

"Of course you do." Toby hunted in his pocket and produced a candy bar. "Sweets for the sweet."

The two girls giggled delightedly and walked with him into the cool and shady hallway of the house.

"Oh good." Molly came out of the study. "You're all together. I—um—wanted to tell you about something—someone—so could you spare me a few minutes?"

"Summer and Ivo aren't back yet," I said, following the others into the living room. "Shouldn't you wait for them?"

"No. I actually want to ask you all a favor in that you won't mention what I'm about to tell you to Ivo *or* Summer."

"But—" I stared at her.

"It's about the old man," she went on rapidly. "The one who startled Sandy the other evening. I *have* asked him to stay away but should he—forget—and any of you spots him, could you just tell me quietly rather than broadcasting it?"

"Why? And why might he forget? Who is he?" Heather asked the questions I wanted answering.

"He's just a poor old local, called Harry, completely harmless but a little confused. He used to come to the house years ago and he doesn't really understand that things have changed. The trouble is, Ivo will take exception to Harry being around, but as he and Summer rarely go into the grounds they're not likely to see him themselves."

"Personally, I think you'd be better telling Ivo about this old man," Hannah said bluntly. "If he's harmless like you say there won't be any problem."

"I think there will. Ivo's already said if Skeet Sanders turns up here uninvited he'll be chased off, and a situation like that would frighten poor old Harry to death. Anyway I could do without Ivo starting up his investigations again. I find it distracting having him feeding names and pictures into that computer of his while I'm trying to teach."

"Pictures? You mean Ivo sends photos to be identified?" Hannah asked.

"Yes. The security firm he works for has access to all sorts of files, he was telling me." Molly wasn't looking directly at her niece as she spoke, so only I noticed the strange, meaningful glance Hannah and Mikey exchanged.

"Oh well, if it's going to cause hassle I'm fine with keeping old Harry a secret," my friend said in a casual, throwaway voice. "How about the rest of you?"

I was sure the petulant Heather would refuse to comply but she and Sandy, still all giggly and girly from Toby's flirting, were in such a good mood they agreed. I could see Sean wasn't too happy about the situation, but in the end we all went along with Molly's request and said we wouldn't make a fuss if we saw Harry around the place. The evening passed totally peacefully with no further sightings as it happened, and the next morning's lesson, with Ivo computer-free, went brilliantly with everyone (except me!) showing great progress with their piece of sculpture.

I just couldn't get the shape I wanted and was still bending and twisting my binding wire while, across from me, Heather was already applying clay to hers. Even in this primitive state her horse was beautiful, from the curve of its neck and spine to the delicate hoof it was lifting in the air. All the other students' pieces were starting to take shape: Birds and heads and geometric forms were growing in their various mediums. It was only on my bench that the wooden base and wire looked—well, like a wooden base and wire. Molly was encouraging as always and told me just to enjoy myself and try to put some "heart and soul into the work," but really I knew that would only happen when I got outside and started riding again.

Buoyed up by the fact Limelight hadn't bolted at Harry's sudden appearance in the field, I was determined to take his training up a notch to see if I could minimize his naughty behavior. Sean agreed it was a good idea and said my pony was ready to extend his range of dressage movements. I'd been hoping for some fast work over much bigger jumps so I made a face.

"That's not the way to do it." He laughed at my sulky expression. "We're building up the bond between you, remember, and the more control you have the better your riding, and better riding—"

"Makes a better horse, yeah, yeah." I yawned. "Okay, after our warm-up and lateral stuff will you show us how to get the perfect flying lead change? Limelight does it naturally when we do the jumping course, but I must be giving the wrong aid on the flat I think."

We worked hard, including work on counter canter to

improve athletic development by giving my pony's left side a stretch workout. Sean told me to ask for a flying change on a twentymeter circle on returning to the side after X, but my horse and I got in a muddle.

"Try a tenmeter circle then a diagonal back to the track, and ask for the change as you head in the new direction," Sean called, but I got it all wrong again.

"I don't think Limelight can do this." I slid off my pony's back and leaned tiredly against him.

"Sure he can. You said yourself he does it easily over fences."

"Can't we just do some jumping then?" I wheedled. "I can't do—"

"Doh! *That's* more like it. It's *you* who's getting it wrong." Sean was being very superior, I thought.

"Well if you're so clever, let's see you get him to do it." I smiled sweetly and handed him the reins.

He swung easily into the saddle and turned Limelight away, moving him round the school through upward and downward transitions, till he had the horse going in a flowing, beautifully collected rhythm.

"Now," he called, "we're going to do our twenty-meter

circle and I want you to pay close attention as we reach X so you can see Limelight produce a perfect flying—"

There was a sudden, shattering explosion, a rapid sequence of shots that rang out somewhere to our right. Limelight, who'd been looking like the perfect example of a model horse, threw up his head, veered sideways, and bolted, running frantically round the school in a panic-stricken gallop. Sean did amazingly well to stay on board, as, thrown out of the saddle, he crouched over my horse's neck, giving and taking with the outside rein. It was the row of little jumps that was their undoing. Although Sean managed to steer the frantic horse away from them on the first three circuits, on the fourth Limelight plunged through the parallels, sending poles crashing and flying around them, making him buck and shy violently. Sean was sent over his head, soaring through the air to land in a horrible tangle of poles and uprights as he totally demolished the second jump.

I leapt from my seat on the fence and ran to him, hoping and praying that he'd be okay, that there'd be some sign of movement from the figure lying frighteningly still facedown in the sand.

Chapter Twelve

When I reached him two amazing things happened. The first was that Limelight, still bolting wildly round the school with reins and leathers flapping, seemed suddenly to catch sight of me and he galloped frantically in my direction. Just as I was about to leap out of his way he skidded to a halt and dropped his nose in my hand.

"He needs you to comfort him." The second miracle was Sean, sitting bolt-upright and *grinning* delightedly at us.

"Com—comfort?" I croaked, stroking my pony's trembling shoulder while I held out my other hand to pull Sean to his feet.

"Yeah." He dusted himself down. "Limelight's terrified of loud noises, bangs, explosions, whatever. That's what sets him off."

"But—" Holding tight to my pony's reins, I thought

about it. "The last time he ran off at home there *was* a shot, it's true, but the other day when we saw Harry on the cliff—"

"Harry dropped a rock down the side of the cliff and it made a loud cracking noise," Sean said, still grinning. "Limelight's not a pony who runs away just for the fun of it. We just have to work on desensitizing him to gunshot-type noises."

"Desensitize?" I did a double take. "Gunshots! Sean, someone was firing a gun—it definitely wasn't a rock being dropped this time!"

"Well, they've stopped now," he pointed out in that calm way of his. "We'll settle Limelight down first then find out what's been going on."

"Are you hurt?" I finally thought to ask.

"Never better," Sean said, suddenly pretending to hobble about. I punched him lightly on the arm, relieved that he'd survived the crash without a scratch.

It took a while for my pony to chill out completely, so while I carried on soothing and quieting I told Sean to go find out about the gunfire.

"There could be some kind of hostage-type siege or battle going on," I said dramatically.

"Doubt it," Sean said cheerfully. "The noise would have lasted a whole lot longer. You keep up the good work with Limelight. It's a great sign that it was you he wanted when he was scared just now—another positive for the bonding process."

I hadn't thought of it like that and felt a glow of satisfaction now that Sean had pointed it out. By the time I was sure my pony had recovered from his fright, checked him over thoroughly, and put him back in the field with his friends, Sean was walking back toward me.

"You won't believe it," he said, quite bitterly for him. "It was only Ivo firing off a round of shots to impress the girls! Heather and Sandy wanted to see what a sure shot he is so he stuck a target on a tree in the garden."

"I hope you told the dumbo what a crazy thing it was to do." I was furious. "You could have been badly hurt— and so could Limelight!"

"Thanks for giving me top billing there." His magical grin was back in place. "He was sort of apologetic, though I don't think he *gets* horses—probably thought I was making a big deal out of nothing."

"Nothing!" I said vengefully. "Wait till Molly hears what he did. Ivo might be big but she'll sort him!"

Molly was indeed "sorting him" as Sean and I approached the garden. I could hear her pointing out forcefully that, scaring horses apart, guns were just not to be fired around Forlorn House.

"It's a peaceful place," she ended.

I heard Sandy mutter, "Oh sure, very peaceful with movie-star daughters and their bodyguards, not to mention mad old men wandering round the grounds!"

I wanted to tell her to shut up, but peace-loving Sean said to leave it.

"Molly's got enough to deal with without us lot fighting among ourselves. Just forget about Ivo—and anyway at least he and his gun are making sure Skeet Sanders doesn't come near the place!"

I hadn't thought of that, but now he'd said it I hoped the firing practice would scare old Harry away too, giving Molly one less thing to worry about. The next couple of days did, in fact, go very peacefully, with no sightings of either man around the grounds or on the cape when we rode out. Molly and Sean started on their desensitizing program with Limelight, getting him used to increasingly loud noises while I continued my herd leader role, staying calm and reassuring my pony everything was fine. In the studio, too, work progressed well and I was at last applying the first layers of wet clay to my armature. My sculpture still looked nothing like a tree, whereas Heather's horse was growing more and more beautiful and the features on Summer's portrait were already unmistakably those of her father.

"Yours is fine," Sean said untruthfully. "It's certainly—dramatic."

"That's one word for it," I said glumly. "*Splodge* is another more accurate one, though."

Sean grinned as he plied a fine chisel on the delicate fronds of his horse's mane.

His woodcarving was gorgeous, and I could see that Hannah's plaster bird was also taking great shape. Even Toby's preoccupation with Summer hadn't stopped him from producing a striking abstract piece. It seemed clear I was turning out to be the class dummy. To be honest, I'd much rather have spent the time on Limelight, but having committed myself to the class and my splodge tree, I felt I ought to stick to it.

"Here you go, Casey." Summer pushed a jar of sweet-smelling lotion toward me after we finished breakfast. "Rub this well into your hands; it protects them from the harsh pigments in the clay."

I dipped my fingers in and rubbed my hands together.

"Your wrists too—take off your watch." She nodded to where the gleaming gold bracelet she wore lay on the table. "That's it—smooth some into your forearms. You too if you like, Heather."

"I'm not bothered, thanks," Heather said ungraciously. "Look, Sandy, Paul's lent me his famous book at last. I might try *ciment fondu* next."

"Take a look at page fourteen." The friendly Summer leaned along the table to show her. "What an illustration, huh!"

We all put our heads together to look at the picture in the book.

"Come on, you lot." Mrs. Fellows, kind but very bossy, was used to chasing us out of the way. "Molly's already in the studio so get yourselves off to class, will you?"

She bustled out of the room to help her assistants, who

were changing bed linens upstairs. All we students rose obediently to our feet and trooped out into the hall. Summer, with Ivo close beside her, led the way followed by Paul and Toby, with Heather and Sandy behind them, while Hannah, Mikey, Sean, and I brought up the rear. I walked over to my bench and stared at my tree, hoping it looked better than I remembered—but it didn't. Heather had already removed the cling film from her horse (it keeps the clay damp and malleable, so I'm told), and I saw Summer do the same with her portrait.

"Oh darn it." She looked down at her bare wrist. "I left my bracelet in the dining room. Ivo, could you go and get it, please?"

"I'll go," Toby said immediately.

Ivo put out a massive hand. "My job, Toby, thanks."

He left the room with the strangely light-footed way he had of moving while I unwrapped my work of art (not!) and got ready to apply another layer of clay. I remember wondering what was taking Ivo so long when he literally burst back into the studio.

"It's gone," he announced flatly. "Summer's gold bracelet has gone!"

"No it can't—it's just there on the table where I was putting my hand cream on." Summer stared at him, shocked.

"I looked on the table, under it, all around. There was no one left in that room, which means someone in this studio must have picked it up."

"A joke you mean?" Summer said uncertainly. "Hey come on, guys, if that's true stop horsing around. That bracelet isn't just gold, it's family. Sentimental, it belonged to my grandmother, so hand it over!"

There was a long, tense silence.

"Does this mean no one has the bracelet?" Molly's voice was tense. "In which case I suggest you search again, Ivo."

"Don't need to do that, ma'am. Searching is something I'm good at. The bracelet is not in that room, so now I need to search this one—and all of you people in it."

"Well really!" Molly was outraged. "You mean you think one of us deliberately took Summer's jewelry?"

"It's valuable money-wise," Ivo said bluntly. "It's part of my job to guard anything belonging to Summer, so if someone's hidden it I need to find it."

Molly reluctantly agreed this was fair comment and accompanied him as he searched every nook and cranny of the studio. The big man was incredibly quick and efficient and soon satisfied himself the bracelet wasn't hidden in any of the drawers or shelves. He then showed Molly how to do a body search, instructing her to perform the same on each of the girls while he frisked all the guys. It didn't take long; under our overalls we were only wearing shorts and T-shirts.

"I hope you're satisfied Mr.—um—Ivo." Molly was flushed and angry looking. "And that you will now apologize to every one of my students."

"Not yet," he said flatly. "The fact remains Summer's bracelet is missing, and only these people here were present when it vanished. The staff were upstairs, nowhere near the dining room, so unless someone else is in or around the house somebody in this room is the guilty party."

"Summer probably left the darn thing in her room," Molly argued.

"No I did not." The beautiful girl was clearly upset. "I wear Grandmother's bracelet every day—just took it off to put on the cream. You saw me, didn't you, Casey?"

I nodded. "You definitely put it on the table. It was there when we all looked at Paul's book."

There were several murmurs of assent.

Molly looked even more harassed. "This is unbelievable! Come on, everyone, back to the dining room and we'll all search this time."

No one had come down to clear the breakfast plates yet so there were plenty of things to pick up and scrutinize, but it was quickly apparent that Ivo's search had been thorough: The slender gold bracelet was nowhere to be found. Summer, although distressed, insisted on carrying on with the morning's class, but there was a distinct atmosphere of unease as we all tried settling back to work. I really couldn't wait to reach Limelight in the afternoon and hugged him tightly, breathing in his wonderful sweet, horsey smell. Hannah had gone to the study to talk to Molly, and it was some time before she came out to join Sean and me.

"My nutty aunt is being nuttier than ever," she announced, clambering bad-temperedly onto the fence. "She's flatly refusing to call the police, says the missing bracelet is 'some kind of mistake' and that it will turn up again."

"Mistake?" I said.

"Turn up?" Sean and I said in unison.

Hannah threw her hands in the air. "I know! Molly's gone stark raving loony if you ask me. I mean *why* doesn't she want the police?"

"I—oh!" A thought struck me. "Does she think Harry took it? She's very protective about him."

"But if the old guy stole the bracelet—" Sean began.

"Molly thinks it was a mistake," I reminded him. "She's always said Harry doesn't mean any harm so maybe she's guessing he picked up the bracelet thinking it was his or something."

"So why doesn't she tell Ivo that?" Hannah wailed. "He's going ballistic—says he could lose his job over this and wants the theft reported at the very least."

"In which case he'll just tell the cops himself, won't he?" Sean shrugged.

"Not yet. Molly made him promise to give her time to sort it out. She hasn't told him about Harry so I don't know how she persuaded Ivo but he's given her twenty-four hours to get the thing back. When she told me I thought she'd just gone batty like I said, but you've probably sussed it— it's Harry she's protecting."

"Maybe we should help her find him," I suggested.

"Molly can't get down to Headley, and I bet the poor old guy doesn't have a phone."

"Toby could go down there on the Harley," Sean said. "He'd take Molly if she wanted."

Molly, still het up and jumpy, at first refused any help.

"It's just a mistake," she kept saying. "Just a silly mistake."

"Maybe so." Toby was serious for once. "But Ivo isn't taking that view. He wants the police in, and when he hears about the weird old man he'll want Summer out—and I don't want that. Let's get this cleared up now."

I knew he was acting mainly on selfish grounds, but it was nice to see the trouble he took getting Molly safely seated on the back of his beloved motorbike.

"I'll be all right as long as you take it steady," she told him. "No racing around the way you usually do."

If we'd been in the mood for laughing it would have been very funny watching speed king Toby potter gently down the coast road. We watched till the big bike was a dot in the distance, then turned away, wandering in desultory fashion back to the garden at the rear.

"What shall we do while we wait?" Paul, always the

quiet one, didn't seem to like the unusual silence.

"I'm going to see Limelight," I said predictably.

He sighed. "That's me excluded, then. I'll go and find the girls."

"You're not excluded. We're trying to get my pony used to sudden noises, so you can be a clatter maker if you like," I said.

"O—kay," he said doubtfully.

Sean, grinning, handed him two saucepan lids. "Equipment for clatter making," he said, trying to raise everyone's spirits. "What about you and Mikey, Hannah? Are you helping with the desensitizing program?"

The two of them had drawn apart and were in deep, whispered conversation.

"Molly said to have Rafferty around. He wouldn't care if a bomb went off, and that will help Limelight." Hannah, looking tense and worried, was making an obvious effort to think about something other than the theft.

"Count me out, guys." Mikey was *really* subdued. "I think I'll go for a run to clear my head a bit."

I saw Hannah bite her lip nervously and wondered why the situation, dire as it was, had created such an air of tension with the pair of them. In contrast Limelight was, for once, in a very laid-back mood and responded well to the sporadic clatter we produced. Rafferty, as usual, just wanted to eat grass, but he stood stoically even when Paul struck his pan lids together more enthusiastically than we wanted, making the hyped-up Hannah nearly fall off with fright. Limelight jumped and skittered too, but listened to my voice and hands, calming quickly without trying to pull away and run from the sharp, explosive sound. We kept the session short as Molly had instructed, and I made a big fuss of my pony before we set him and Rafferty loose in their paddock. Hannah, still withdrawn and anxious look-ing, was plodding back to the tack room with her saddle when all hell, in the shape of Heather and Sandy, broke loose.

"Thought we'd find you here!" They sounded tri-umphant. "Oh—where's *Mikey?*"

"Gone for a run." Hannah stood very still. "Why?"

"Because Ivo wants a word. He has a problem." Heather turned back toward the house.

"Why?" Hannah, now quite pale, said again.

"Ivo's been doing more research, that's why." Sandy, who

always seemed to enjoy a crisis, pulled a comic face. "He's been asking for identity photos of the students this time, and it seems Mikey isn't who he says he is."

"What are you implying—that he's some kind of crook?" Sean snapped angrily.

"No way!" Paul was mad too. "If Ivo thinks Mikey stole Summer's bracelet there's just no way—"

"They're not listening," I butted in. "Too busy rushing back to tell Ivo where Mikey's gone."

"I've got to warn him!" Hannah pushed her pony's tack at Sean and started running. "Danny!" she called, her voice becoming fainter as she left the yard behind. "Da-a-n-n-y!"

Sean, Paul, and I stood frozen to the spot and gaped at each other. Just what was going on *now* and who the heck was Danny?

Chapter Thirteen

Hannah was gone so long I began to think she'd literally done a runner and left. We hung round the yard for a while waiting for her, then agreed we ought to make an appearance at the house in case Ivo thought we'd all taken off, too. He was ensconced in the studio, tapping away at the keys of his laptop while Summer worked on the life-like clay portrait of her father. She'd built the clay up in textured layers, giving Matt Fenton's features a rugged, craggy look. When Sean, Paul, and I walked into the room she looked up, smiled briefly, then bent her head to concentrate on the sculpture again. I guessed that working the clay soothed her in the way being with Limelight did for me. Ivo, however, looked particularly unsoothed.

"Where is he?" His voice, still quiet, held a new menace.

"Hannah's gone to find him," I replied. "What's all this about, Ivo?"

He turned the computer screen toward us. "Know who this is?"

A young man's face looked out at us, vaguely familiar but not instantly identifiable.

We all shook our heads doubtfully.

Ivo bared his teeth in a humorless grin. "Strange that, seeing as this is a picture of Mikey Owens, student at Molly Renshaw's first summer school."

"What new nonsense is this?" We hadn't heard Molly arrive, but she made her presence felt now. "And who said you could use my studio as some kind of interrogation chamber?"

"Hang on, Molly." Summer stopped with her hands on her father's fine cheekbones. "Ivo's only doing his job."

"I still don't want him and that computer in here," Molly snapped back. "What's this rubbish about that picture being Mikey?"

"I asked for photographic data of everyone in the house," Ivo said evenly. "They all match except for this one. This is the real Mikey Owens, aged nineteen, of Allerton, Liverpool, winner of this year's Tressant Art Scholarship."

"Those are certainly the qualifications he gave when he applied." Molly squinted closely at the screen. "I must say I've been disappointed in his work so far—it's adequate but doesn't have the spark you'd expect from a Tressant winner."

I gave a shudder of dismay. "So Mikey—the Mikey we know—is an imposter?"

"Yeah, I'd say so. And I need to know why." Ivo sounded impossibly tough.

"I don't see it's any of your business," Sean said, rather surprisingly. "I mean, what does it matter to you if the kid pretended to be someone else in order to get a place here?"

Ivo blinked but recovered quickly. "My priority's protecting Summer, and I have to think maybe he did it to get access to her."

"Rubbish!" I joined in. "Molly didn't even accept Summer as a student till *after* we were all here."

Ivo's shoulders twitched uncomfortably. "He may have heard a rumor she was applying—look, you heard Molly say the kid's no great shakes as a sculptor, so that wasn't the reason he lied to get in here."

I had no answer to that and, remembering how "Mikey"

had been so dismayed at the thought of Ivo making inquiries about him he'd actually fallen off the gate, I was starting to feel very, very worried. I wouldn't have blamed Mikey and Hannah for staying well away but ten minutes later they walked in together, heads high and holding hands.

"Hello, Molly." Hannah touched her aunt's shoulder hesitantly. "More trouble, I'm afraid."

"So I believe." Molly looked at them both. "Aren't you going to introduce your friend?"

"I'm Danny—Danny Owens. Mikey's my older brother." His gaze was very clear and direct. "I'm sorry we deceived you but I swear it was nothing to do with Summer *or* her bracelet. I might be a phony but I'm not a thief."

"You're not a sculptor either," Molly said drily. "But I don't suppose that's an indictable offense."

Danny gave a faint grin. "Mikey said I'd never get away with it with you, but I gave it my best shot."

"So if it's your brother's who's got the talent, why didn't he come along himself?" Summer raised her clay-covered hands in exasperation. "Do you guys just like making life difficult or something?"

"Seems like that. The reason's a girl of course—the most beautiful girl in the world according to my brother. He met her after he got accepted at Molly's but our parents didn't like her far-out lifestyle and said he had to honor his booking here and not join her in Glastonbury. I was due to spend the vacation at summer camp so we worked out between us that I'd cancel my booking there and instead take Mikey's place, leaving him free to visit his hippie girlfriend. I ring him and tell him what's happening here so he can ring our parents and relay it to them."

"And if they call you on your cell phone you pretend to be at summer camp! Good one, Mikey—I mean Danny!" Sean thought it was dead funny, but Ivo didn't share his point of view.

"It's a neat enough story, but the fact remains you're not the person you claimed to be. And that puts you high on my list of suspects."

"Suspects? Why? Check out Danny Owens, aged sixteen, of Allerton, Liverpool, on your darn computer. I'm no more a thief than my brother, so how come I'm Public Enemy Number One as far as you're concerned?"

"He's right. And you searched him yourself when the

bracelet went missing, didn't you, Ivo? Where is—er—Danny supposed to have hidden the thing?" Paul, having stayed quiet, now had plenty to say. "Come on then, mister, you're the one paid to observe everything that happens around Summer, so why don't you describe the sequence of events this morning?"

"Sure," the bodyguard said after a short pause. "Why not? We finished breakfast. Summer took off her bracelet and started applying cream, offering it to Casey who was sitting opposite and Heather, seated two seats along, who refused. Heather opened up Paul's book and Sandy, Toby, Hannah, Sean, Casey, and Mikey looked at the page pointed out by Summer. Mrs. Fellows told everyone to shift, then she left the room. I checked the hall, which was empty, and led the way to the studio, with Summer beside me, followed by Paul and Toby, then Heather and Sandy, and finally Hannah, Mikey, Sean, and Casey in a group. The breakfast dishes were still on the table, as well as Paul's book, which was picked up by Heather. The window of the dining room was open but no one had the chance to go to it or throw the bracelet out without one of the other students noticing. Anyone could have secretly palmed it but no one had chance to hide it except on their person, in the dining room, in the studio, or in the hall, all of which I searched. Or in Paul's book, but I checked that too."

He rattled this off in a flat, expressionless voice. We all blinked and looked at each other.

"Er—very efficient, but you seem to be saying any one of us *could* have taken the thing but none of us did?" Danny, as I guess we had to get used to calling him, sounded bewildered.

"Unless two or more of you are in cahoots—working together as a team," Ivo said.

Molly threw up her hands in protest. "Oh really, is that likely? I mean, if any one of them *did* steal Summer's bracelet, it was hardly a premeditated plan—so when would this conspiracy have been arranged?"

Ivo's response was to shrug his massive shoulders. "It's just a theory. I have others."

"You do? And what are they, I wonder? That someone trained a bird, a magpie or maybe a crow, to swoop through the open window and fly off with any nice bit of jewelry left lying around?" Molly's temper was on a very short fuse, but the bodyguard seemed impervious.

"No, that's not one. You might be able to help after your trip to Headley earlier. What did Harry Mason have to say?"

"Harry?" Now Molly looked really mad. "Who's been telling tales about the poor old man?"

"Nobody. You didn't really think I wouldn't check up on an old guy hanging around the place, did you? As soon as I spotted him I ran his details through immediately. Because his connection was with you and your father's shipwreck I didn't think him a threat. General consensus of opinion is that he's a harmless old fool."

"I find the description insulting but I'm glad you agree he means no harm." Molly controlled her passion with an obvious effort. "I—I went to see him today to make sure he'd kept his promise and stayed away from Forlorn House."

"You thought he must have done it," Ivo said shrewdly. "And you went to ask for the bracelet back so you could smooth it over."

"If she did there was no need," Toby joined in hotly. "Harry doesn't have many words. He's had a bang on the head and finds it hard to communicate, but he made it clear he'd been nowhere near the bracelet. Nowhere near Forlorn House, in fact."

"I'm afraid, you know, that last statement definitely isn't true." Sandy, agog as usual to be part of the action, had just showed up. "Heather didn't want to say anything at first because we promised Molly we wouldn't but it's different now. *Harry was here in the grounds, right outside the house, when we came down to breakfast today!*"

I couldn't look at Molly—how on earth was she going to react at hearing Harry had lied to her, which in turn meant he was surely the thief as well? Her reaction, predictably, was one of complete denial.

"Nonsense. You two have muddled up the days or something. You live in your own selfish little world too much to notice anything."

"Excuse *me*!" Sandy was very put out. "If we're doing personal mudslinging, you're the one living in a parallel universe, Molly Renshaw—ignoring ghost sightings, threats from locals, and unexplained accidents! If you're not living in Forlorn House's past, why do you put up with Harry wandering round the place and why tell us all we're to keep him secret?"

Molly, her face sheet white, gripped her walking stick so hard I was afraid she'd strike the girl with it.

"The answer,"—Ivo's quiet, emotionless voice cut through the charged atmosphere—"is that Harry Mason was the other survivor from the wreck of the *Lady Fair*. He was hauled out of the sea by rescuers but he was badly hurt and his mind was gone. That's why Molly defends him the way she does."

"Yes that's right." Molly threw back her head and faced us. "I feel guilty—responsible—that's why I don't want him hunted down this way. I knew Harry while I was growing up and he was a sweet, good man. A blow on the head doesn't change that—he is innocent and I won't have him arrested."

"But Molly—what about my bracelet?" Summer spoke gently. "If it was just money I'd leave it, seeing as you care so much, but the bracelet's *my* family history. It's as important to me as anything in your past is to you."

I could see her words had made an impact on everyone. I felt so sorry for Molly as one by one they muttered that Summer was right.

"The police will tread carefully with Harry, there won't

be any bullying," Toby said.

Sean nodded. "You have to tell them about him, Molly."

"No." Her eyes blazed. "I do not. I'm truly, truly sorry about Summer's bracelet but I will not have Harry arrested."

Her lower lip trembled, and she turned away to hobble blindly from the room.

I swallowed hard and said, "I think I'm the only one to agree with her. I don't think the old guy did it either, and if he's ill he should be left alone."

"Oh come on, Casey." Hannah looked drained. "Molly's completely irrational; you don't have to defend her."

"It's academic anyway," Paul put in. "Ivo's going to have to report the theft to the police; it's not Molly's decision to make."

"Yeah, guess so," Sean said.

Wound up beyond endurance, I turned on him. "So that's it then? You're deserting Molly, all of you, after all she's been through? We should be loyal like she is and back her up, not help knock her down this way."

"Simmer down, Casey," Hannah said wearily. "It's not

your fight."

"Maybe not." I knew she was finding my reaction over-the-top, but I felt so strongly I just couldn't stop. "But it should be yours. I know I'm not family but from now on it's Molly, Harry, and me against the lot of you!"

The feeling of injustice had been building up inside. I ran from the studio with a desperate need to put physical space between me and the people I'd thought were Molly's friends.

Chapter Fourteen

I headed, of course, straight for Limelight, wanting only to put my arms round him and sob into his warm, comforting shoulder. The sudden rush of emotion I felt had taken me by surprise, and when I saw Molly limping determinedly in the direction of the paddock, my heart sank. I really didn't want to talk, there'd been too much of that already, but I thought she needed to know someone was on her side. When I caught up with her I slowed my pace and walked alongside.

"Are you going to see Mac and Ozzie?"

She nodded abruptly. "I'll get more sense from them."

"That's how I feel." I took a deep breath. "Ivo's going to report the theft to the police *and* tell them about Harry."

"You all think that's all right, do you?" She wouldn't look at me.

"*I* don't and I've said so."

"Thank you for that, Casey." She raised her eyes to mine. "But the others—my niece, Toby and Sean whom I've known for years—they simply consider I'm being madder than usual trying to defend Harry this way."

"I think they just want the whole thing cleared up. It's a horrible feeling wondering if one of us is a thief, so they'd prefer it to be an outsider."

"I can understand them wanting it to be an outsider, but not that poor old man! I can't expect you to understand—"

"I think I do," I said quickly. "I was dead-set against Harry, wasn't I—thinking him a nuisance and a weirdo—but when I saw how upset he was about spooking Limelight I could see he doesn't have a mean bone in his body. I can't believe he'd do something deliberately wicked."

"I firmly believe he's incapable of that," Molly said, nodding eagerly. "Harry was one of my father's crew for many, many years. He wasn't—terribly bright—but honest, kind, and hardworking. I knew he'd been injured in the shipwreck but we moved away almost immediately and it wasn't till I came back I discovered he's lost all his memory and much of his speech."

"No wonder you feel so protective toward him." We were now walking across to the group of horses in the paddock. "Isn't there anything we can do?"

Molly put her arm round Ozzie who'd come over to nuzzle her. "If I didn't have this wretched injury I'd ride this boy of mine out onto the cape to see if I could find Harry. He was terribly upset by my visit, you know, Casey, and when he's distressed he goes off to stare at the sea."

"I've seen him do that." I hesitated, wanting desperately to help but scared of the possible consequences. "I—I could ride Limelight and go look for him. Harry knows me; I might be able to calm him so he's at least prepared for the police visit."

"You'd do that?" Molly looked really touched. "But you're still nervous about riding out on your own. Limelight can be tricky, I know."

"He's much better than he was." I hugged my pony's silver neck. "Anyway it's important to reach Harry before he gets frightened so I want to do it."

"You're brilliant, Casey. I can't think why you're being so supportive to a cranky woman like me but I appreciate it, I promise you."

"You're not so bad," I said, trying to lighten the mood. "In fact, in normal circumstances I'd say you were pretty darn good!"

"Normal!" She grinned ruefully. "I've forgotten what life's like when it's normal!"

It didn't take long to brush Limelight and get him saddled up and ready. Molly told me to stick to the path at the very edge of the cliff.

"It's where you're most likely to spot Harry, and you can't go fast along it. That will lessen the likelihood of Limelight bombing off."

I bit my lip at the thought and she immediately said, "You don't have to do this, Casey. I can call a cab and go wait outside Harry's house till he gets home."

"If he's upset he could spend all day on the cape." I made myself relax and smile at her. "I'll be fine; Limelight's practically a model horse already."

"Don't get me started on models," Molly snorted as she tightened my girth. "What with Mikey not being Mikey, I've already got his rubbishy metallic figure spoiling my studio, and now Heather's horse that looked so promising is starting to look like a deformed camel."

"Never mind." I swung into the saddle and grinned down at her. "There's always my tree—art or what!"

"I think I'd have to say 'what'!" She grinned back. "You might not be a sculptor, but you have other far better qualities, Casey."

High praise indeed. I just hoped I wasn't going to mess up and spoil her opinion. Limelight was eager to get going and didn't seem to mind being without his equine companions for once. He walked out well until he was nicely warmed up, then moved smoothly into working trot when I asked. I was concentrating on keeping relaxed, keeping a sharp lookout for Harry, and keeping my horse under control. Limelight pulled hard when we cantered on a short uphill stretch but dropped the pace obediently as I slowed to peer down the side of the cliff. We were nearing the horses' beach and I really hoped I'd spot Harry down there. The lovely bay was empty, though, with just a few gulls swooping above the clear turquoise water as it lapped gently, endlessly on the shore. The track was becoming wilder and rockier, and my horse had to concentrate on picking his way carefully between the boulders strewn along the way. Once, his hooves dislodged a big pebble, sending it rolling and crashing down the side of the cliff on a sheer drop to the ocean. The noise startled Limelight and he shivered, the muscles in his neck twitching rapidly as he turned his head anxiously toward the sound.

"It's okay, baby," I crooned in that soppy, soothing way of mine. "Nothing to worry about. Walk on."

His ears flickered as I spoke and he visibly relaxed, moving forward obediently. I sighed with relief and kept searching, scanning every crag and ledge of the sheer cliffs below us. I wondered about calling Harry's name but thought it might scare him into hiding, so Limelight and I just kept going, steadily, patiently, and silently. We reached the farthest point of the cape, the exposed headland where Sean had pointed to the rocky outcrop jutting out into the sea below. Today the tide was coming in; I could see the line of waves sweeping in strongly on their journey to the beach. Already they were slapping against the farthest rock, sending white plumy showers skyward as they broke one by one against the jagged slate.

It was then I saw him, lying stretched on his back, arms flung out to his sides with one leg straight while the other was bent at an odd angle beneath it. For once the hood was not drawn over his head; the light glinted on his thinning gray hair and full bushy beard. For one idiotic moment I thought he was sunbathing, lying on the long, flattish rock for pleasure. Then the cold realization hit that he wasn't moving, not reacting in the slightest as the incoming tide surged its relentless way toward him. Instinctively I fumbled in my pocket for my cell phone, feeling another sickening lurch as my fingers met nothing. I hadn't intended coming out, of course; I'd left my phone in the house and would now have to ride like the wind to get help.

I looked down at the rock again, willing Harry to make a move. I felt sure I saw the rise and fall of his chest as he breathed, but the only real change was with the ocean, rolling nearer and nearer to the shore. I figured it would cover the end rock in less than five minutes, which meant only ten more before the waves were breaking over the inert, pathetic figure of the old man. I had no choice: Somehow I had to scramble down the cliff and get to Harry before the tide did. The cliff looked impossibly sheer, dropping away from Limelight's hooves in a series of craggy vertical slabs. If I got off Limelight and sat on my butt I could maybe slide—

I leaned forward to judge the descent, inadvertently squeezing my pony's sides, and he responded instantly, taking small, neat steps along a minuscule trail between the great granite slabs. I gasped, then tried to relax, giving him a loose rein and leaning back in the saddle to help his balance. It took him nearly six minutes to pick his way carefully, accurately down the side of the cliff. When he at last walked forward onto the ledge of sand at its foot he gave himself a shake as if to unwind every tensed muscle in his body. The beach, shaped by centuries of pounding seas, had been molded into three distinct levels. The highest, at the cliff base where we stood, was seaweed-free, being beyond the reach of the incoming tide, and therefore safe. Level two was covered in shells and ocean debris, and the waves were already curling and lapping at the upper edge of the third. Farther out the end rock had disappeared, lost under the waves that now pounded and splashed ominously around the long, flat outcrop where Harry lay. I could swim out to reach him—but what then? The old man was thin and didn't look heavy, but he was tall and, being obviously unconscious, would be a deadweight, too much for me to hold above water. My only chance was

Limelight, a horse who'd never been deeper than hock level in any water and who I'd intended coaxing and reassuring into a calm ocean in the bay one day.

"Sorry, Limelight." I leaned forward and kissed his ears. "It's got to be here and now, I'm afraid."

Quickly I stripped off his saddle and my jeans. Vaulting onto his bare back I pushed him forward across the second ridge of sand onto the firm damp texture at the water's edge. We were heading at a diagonal, cutting through the shallows and getting deeper and deeper as we approached the outcrop of rocks. Limelight hesitated when the waves broke around his knees, but my role as herd leader had never been so vital and I urged him on, feeling a thrill of exultance as he began cresting his way through the turbulent water. And then we were swimming, the ocean swirling over his back as he struck out vigorously. My legs, curved firmly round his sleek sides, felt the pull of the strong tide in this exposed headland, and as Limelight swam against its flow I felt a huge surge of pride in my pony despite the horror of the situation. The sea already covered half the long rock and was sweeping forward again and again to lap round the heel of Harry's right boot. His breathing seemed normal and even but his eyes remained closed, and he didn't react to the first cold touch of the ocean as it swirled around his stretched-out leg.

The other leg bothered me, probably broken, would I do more damage by moving him?—but again the sea made up my mind, surging forward to cover his knees. If I didn't do something there'd be no leg to save so, holding tightly to Limelight's reins with one hand, I slid from his back onto the half-submerged rock and leaned toward the old man. This time the ocean was a help, buoying up his body so I had no weight to take. I supported Harry's head, lifesaver-style, and pulled his shoulders firmly toward us, floating him in as straight a line as I could to my bravely swimming horse. By a sheer fluke I managed it in one, hauling Harry through the shallow water on the rock and maneuvering him from its ledge onto Limelight's back.

My poor horse snorted and showed the whites of his eyes but I now swam alongside him, talking calmly to convince him it was okay. I'm a good swimmer but could only use my legs, both hands being taken up with guiding Limelight and keeping Harry on board. Several times, despite my strong kicking, the waves broke over my head, forcing me to swallow great gulps of sharp, salty water. It was an exhausting, terrifying journey back to shore, and I used every ounce of strength I possessed. Somehow, against what must have been impossible odds, we made it and I staggered from the sea, leading my tired, brave, *wonderful* pony and his still-unconscious cargo. When we reached the ledge of dry sand at the cliff base I leaned against a rock, my breath rasping in my chest and the blood thundering so loudly in my ears that it was several moments before I heard the cry.

"Casey—CASEY!" The voice was Sean's and I let out a sob when I heard, too, the unmistakable roar of the Harley on the cliff above us.

Within minutes Sean was on the strip of beach, his strong arms around me, holding me from falling as I slumped, exhausted, against him.

"We've phoned for help—it's already on its way—my God, Casey, we saw what you did, you were wonderful!"

"I've probably killed Harry—" I gasped as I sank gratefully to the sand.

"No, you've saved his life!" Sean lifted Harry from Limelight's back and lowered him gently, checking him over rapidly. "They'll take him straight to hospital—you'd better go too and get checked out."

"No, I'm fine." I managed a smile and added, very politely, "The trouble is I don't think I can make it back up that cliff," before blacking out in a complete and utter dead faint.

Chapter Fifteen

I'd never fainted in my life before and always thought it sounded a highly dramatic thing to do. In reality, though, it's kind of—nothing. I honestly don't remember a thing till I woke up in a very white bed in a very white hospital ward. Sean said later the cliff rescue was like something from an action movie, but I missed it all. I didn't mind not knowing the bit when the paramedics cleared my insides of what looked to Sean like several gallons of seawater, but I'd have liked to see Harry, strapped up securely, being winched up the side of the cliff. He wasn't conscious for any of it either so I guess he had the same experience of nothingness.

Excitingly, there was big, *big* news when he finally did come to. Molly, alerted by Sean and Toby, had been waiting at the hospital before Harry and I even arrived, and stayed at my side until she was satisfied I was going to be completely fine. She then limped away to find out about Harry, who'd been taken to a different ward. He took longer to regain consciousness, which was probably a good thing as his broken leg and several lacerations were dealt with before he came round. Molly was gone for ages, but being praised and fussed over by my friends, who wanted to know every last detail of my "swim from hell," I hadn't given it much thought. When she hobbled back toward us, though, I knew something fantastic had happened. Molly, like her niece Hannah, has a smile that can light up a room, an engaging gap-toothed beam that makes everyone on the receiving end smile back. The smile hadn't been much in evidence since we'd arrived at Forlorn House, so it was a wonderful sight to see.

"How come you're grinning like an idiot, Molly?" was the down-to-earth Hannah's take on it.

"Idiot yourself." Molly pretended to clout her with her stick. "I was double-triple-quadruple delighted when I heard Casey had rescued Harry but now—well, you can multiply that by a million!"

"Good news? You've found Summer's bracelet, have you?" Toby sat up expectantly.

Molly waved the stick at him too. "Heck no—*much* better than that! Harry's bumped and battered but he'll mend and—get this—somehow one of the bumps has restored his memory!"

"No!" We all gasped in unison.

She nodded, suddenly serious and obviously emotional. "He doesn't remember how he ended up on that rock today and he's still a bit groggy but he's now got total recall of the night the *Lady Fair* was wrecked. Listen to this!" She gulped and took a deep breath. "It wasn't my father's fault! Harry says Andrew Renshaw liked a drink but never *ever* when he was in charge of the boat and *it wasn't him at the wheel when she foundered off the cape.*"

"Don't tell me." Despite being the one in the hospital bed I was quicker than the others. "Skeet Sanders. It was Skeet Sanders's fault."

She nodded. "*Skeet* was the one who'd been drinking. When my father realized it, he tried to wrench the *Lady Fair* away from the rocks, but it was too late. Harry says Captain Renshaw died trying to save everyone on board— can—can you believe that!"

Her eyes, unnaturally bright, were full of tears.

Hannah, also crying, flung her arms around her aunt. "*You* believed in him always, didn't you Molly?"

"Wow!" Sean was deeply impressed. "What a story! No wonder Harry spent so much time wandering the cape. Without consciously knowing it he must have been searching for the truth all these years."

"Seeing Hannah would have struck a chord somewhere," Toby said slowly. "Harry must have struggled to understand she wasn't the fifteen-year-old Molly he used to know. Are you going to take Skeet Sanders to court, Molly? With Harry's evidence there's no doubt he'd be found guilty."

"Just knowing for sure my father was innocent is enough at the moment," Molly said quietly. "When Harry's fully recovered I'll see what he wants to do and of course back him all the way."

"It's a happy ending." I beamed at them all from my now rumpled white bed. "For the Renshaw family and Forlorn House, for Harry and for me and my amazing model horse!"

"Who, as I've told you a thousand times, is absolutely fine," Sean said, ruffling my hair affectionately. "Unlike you, he didn't swallow half the ocean!"

We were all on a high, laughing and talking except Toby, who said bleakly, "I hate to spoil the party but it's not exactly a happy end for some, is it? I mean, not an end at all when it comes to the other mystery at Forlorn House."

"Other? Oh, you mean Summer's bracelet," Molly said reluctantly. "Well, I still say Harry's not guilty. His recent memories are vague at present but even if Sandy and Heather were right and he was hanging round the house when the thing disappeared, he didn't take it. I stake my life on that."

"Well, *someone* took it," Toby argued. "So that someone has got to be one of the students. Ivo said it was perfectly possible for any one of us."

"In which case, where's the darn thing hidden?" Molly was exasperated. "Of course we have to find it—as Summer very fairly pointed out, the bracelet is part of her own family history and I *know* how important that is. Come on, you lot, apply some brainpower. You might not all be sculptors—I'm looking at you here, Mikey-I-mean-Danny—but you're all fairly bright, aren't you?"

"Obviously not." Danny smiled slightly warily at her.

"Honest, Molly, I've racked my brains to think of some-where the bracelet could be hidden without Ivo the search engine finding it. I'm working hard to get brownie points with you to make up for the fact I've got no talent."

I thought of the distorted lump of clay that was my tree and smiled inwardly, almost flinching as something went *click* inside my brain. What was it Molly had said about our sculptures when she referred to them spoiling her studio? It was no good; the thought, elusive as the spray on a windblown wave, vanished. I had to stay in hospital overnight so the doctors could satisfy themselves I was 100 percent, and when I walked into Forlorn House the next morning the first thing I saw was a row of suitcases.

"Hi, honey." Summer wafted over and kissed my cheek. "I hung on to say good-bye, Casey. You turned out be a genuine hero, didn't you?"

"Nah." I'd had enough of all that. "I'm just happy I got Limelight in for a swim at last, that's all. Why are you leaving?"

"I don't have any choice. I had to tell Pop about the bracelet and he's furious, so he wants me home right away."

"And we're going too." Sandy had a very righteous look

on her face. "We think Molly was totally out of line defending that strange old man and we're quitting her school as a mark of solidarity with Summer."

"*Solidarity with Summer?*" I scoffed. "I doubt it! And the old man, as you call him, didn't steal the thing. I'm not convinced you saw him outside the window yesterday." I was stung into retaliation by her smugness. "You're quite sure about that, are you?"

"Heather is, certainly," she said, backing off. "I didn't actually see him, but she told me about it."

I felt another resounding *click*, like a light switch going on in my brain. This time I knew what it meant.

"Heather," I said carefully. "Ah."

The tall, thin girl came into the room, carrying the still-damp sculpture of her horse. Although patently no artist I could see exactly what Molly had meant. The once pure lines of the horse were distorted; the layers of clay, instead of following the perfect, delicate outline of the torso, were lumpy and uneven.

"You're taking your work of art I see, Heather," I said pleasantly.

She flushed. "What's it to you? Ivo's giving us a lift to the bus terminal so I might as well carry it."

"Pleased with it are you?" I leaned forward to touch the model horse.

She jerked it out of reach. "Leave it, Casey, it still has to dry."

"Mm, especially where you've piled the clay on in those thick lumps—" I leapt forward and knocked the horse violently from her hands, sending it flying through the air. It landed on the tiles at Ivo's feet, smashing and crumbling into a thousand damp clay pieces. The bodyguard looked first at me, then Heather, in complete astonishment and then lowered his gaze to the floor. There, amid the debris of wood, wire, and clay, gleamed Summer's gold bracelet, the pure morning light of Cape Forlorn burnishing its delicate links to flame. Heather screamed and ran at me, fingers curved into talons, but Sean stepped between us and easily pinned her clawing hands behind her. I'm sorry to say I quite enjoyed myself, particularly when I saw the smug, self-righteous expression wiped clean off Sandy's pretty little features as she gaped, openmouthed, at her writhing, cursing friend.

"So how did you *know*? And when? And—?" It was later and Sean was torn between hugging me and asking a million questions. I must say I preferred the hugs.

"It was Molly's comment about Heather's model horse looking more like a camel," I explained. "Although I thought the sculpture's odd shape was artistic interpretation and didn't make the connection at the time. When Sandy announced it was only *Heather* who supposedly saw Harry outside the house I realized she'd set him up, and it clicked where the bracelet was hidden. Heather scooped it up underneath Paul's book as we left the dining room—a complete impulse, but I'd say she was a practiced thief, wouldn't you? When Ivo went to look for the thing Heather had more sense than to draw attention to herself by leaving the studio to hide it. She merely slapped it onto her sculpture under a hefty dollop of clay. She probably meant to retrieve it sometime but Summer and Ivo were always in and out of the studio so it was safer to leave it where it was. Implicating Harry by saying she'd seen him was a real dirty trick but—"

"But then Heather's a real dirty character." Summer stroked her cleaned-up bracelet. "Thanks, Casey, darling, not just for my grandmother's memory, but for me too. Now I can stay on and start learning everything Molly Renshaw can teach me."

"Oh joy!" the wicked Molly muttered, raising her eyebrows as Summer and her bodyguard moved away.

"Don't pretend to be cynical. You're as pleased as we are that she's staying." Toby and Paul gave her a nudge.

"She's talented, I grant you." Molly gave them the usual tap with her stick. "But I can't possibly be as happy as you two love-struck goons!"

They drifted away, joking and arguing, and were soon joined by Hannah and Danny. Sean and I could hear them all laughing way after they'd gone out of sight, and I thought how great it was that the atmosphere at Forlorn House had now lifted and blossomed.

"You're even prettier when you're happy." Sean gently tweaked my nose. "D'you think in a day or two when you've both recovered from all that heroism, Rifka and I could go swimming with you and Limelight?"

"It's a date." I smiled back, and that was the *real* start of the vacation Limelight and I will never forget.

JENNY HUGHES lives in Dorset, England. She has written twenty-two horse novels for young adults, which have been published in eight countries. Jenny's books are based on her experience working at a farm, at a riding school, and with polo ponies; but most of all they spring from her deep love of horses and the joy of sharing her life with such amazing beings.